MR. HUNT, I PRESUME

A PLAYFUL BRIDES STORY

VALERIE BOWMAN

JUNE THIRD ENTERPRISES, LLC

Print edition ISBN: 978-0-9893758-2-5

Digital edition ISBN: 978-0-9893758-1-8

Book Cover Design © Lyndsey Lewellen at Llewellen Designs.

For my aunt, Susan Hammond Spitz, who is also a writer and a fantastic wit. With love.

ACKNOWLEDGMENTS

Thank you to Shelby Reed, Kim Kenealy, and Candice Davis for helping make this book the best it could be.

CHAPTER ONE

London, August 1824

Lucy Hunt stared at the looming stack of letters that sat on the writing desk in front of her. She shook her head. "How in the world am I to go through all of these?"

Her husband, Derek, the Duke of Claringdon, strolled up behind her to peer over her shoulder. "What are they?"

"Inquiries for employment. There must be a hundred of them."

"For the governess position?" Derek asked.

"Yes. I'm quite overwhelmed."

"Don't worry. I'll help you choose some to meet with." He cleared his throat and picked up the first sheet of vellum from the stack. "Mrs. Harriet Kindlewood. Previously employed for fifty years by the Marquess of Dorset."

"Fifty years?" Lucy exclaimed. "Why the poor woman must be at least seventy! She should be pensioned off by now."

Discarding the first letter, Derek picked up the next one.

"Miss Patience Horville. Clean, punctual, not afraid to discipline unruly children no matter how young."

Lucy shuddered. "Ralph and Mary are only two and three. I'm not certain how much discipline they need. Besides, I've found that when someone has a name such as Patience, she usually has none of it."

"At least she's clean and punctual," Derek replied with a laugh.

Lucy sat back and blew out a breath. "Be serious, Derek. I've been at my wits' end since Miss Langley left. She was such an excellent governess."

Derek pressed his lips together. "Yes. It's a pity she had to go fall in love and get married."

Lucy crossed her arms over her chest and arched her brow to return his stare. "It's not a pity at all. I played a significant role in making her match with Mr. Benton. It's only a pity that she had to move away and leave us."

A smile crept to Derek's face. "Perhaps if you and Delilah Montebank weren't always trying to matchmake everyone, we would have a governess with a longer tenure. Where did all these letters come from, at any rate?"

"I asked all my friends for references, but none of them had anyone. Hence, I reached out to Mrs. Griggs's employment office. Her services come highly recommended."

"There's no help for it then," Derek replied. "We'll just have to go through all of these and pick a few to meet with."

With a sigh, Lucy grabbed the next letter from the top and read it aloud. "Miss Erienne Stone, formerly of Brighton, currently of London. Gently reared woman seeks position as governess. Able to teach reading, writing, and maths as well as French, history, and globes. Trained in music, art, needlework, and deportment. Caring and kind. Strict when necessary. Excellent references available."

"Erienne Stone?" Derek frowned. "Did you say formerly of Brighton?"

"Yes." Lucy lowered the paper to the desk. "You don't know her, do you?" Derek had been born and raised in Brighton before he'd gone into his majesty's army and rose through the ranks to fight at Waterloo. He'd been made a duke for his efforts.

"It must be a coincidence," he replied, shaking his head.

"How did you know her?" Lucy asked.

"She was the daughter of a knight. Sir Robert Stone. She grew up with us. Only she was of a much better stature than my poor family."

"Was she kind to you? She didn't look down upon you, did she?" Lucy asked.

"To the contrary. In fact, she and Collin…" Derek's voice drifted off. He rubbed his chin as if deep in thought. "Nevermind. It cannot possibly be the same woman. She would have to be at least thirty years old by now, and at any rate, I'm almost certain the Miss Stone I knew married well and moved to Shropsbury."

Lucy's different-colored eyes sparkled. "Wait a moment. What were you going to say? About she and Collin?"

Collin was Derek's middle brother. The two of them, along with their youngest brother, Adam, had grown up the sons of an army veteran who insisted all three boys join the military. Derek and Collin had actually enjoyed it. Even after the wars ended, Collin, who had been a spy for the War Office, had remained in the army and was now a general. Adam, however, was currently happily employed as a publisher and even more happily married to his wife, Cecelia. But Collin was a confirmed bachelor at the age of five and thirty, which drove Lucy, a dedicated matchmaker, a bit mad.

"I wasn't going to say anything about Miss Stone and

Collin," Derek replied in a guarded tone. "They courted, I think. It was nothing serious."

Lucy widened her eyes. "They courted? Are you quite serious? I've never known Collin to court anyone." She snatched up the letter from Miss Stone and stared at it anew. Her brow furrowed. "Wait a moment! This isn't the same woman who …"

"What?"

Lucy tapped her cheek, desperately trying to remember details of a conversation that had taken place many years ago. "I asked Collin once why he seemed so bent on refusing to marry."

"He didn't answer you, did he?" Derek paced toward the fireplace, crossing his arms over his chest.

"On the contrary, he was quite deep in his cups that evening, which is rare for Collin, and which is also why I sought him out and asked him that particular question on that particular evening."

Derek shook his head and gave his wife a vague grin as if she was perfectly incorrigible. "Because you thought you'd have a better chance of getting a response from him?"

"Precisely," Lucy said. "And an honest one."

Derek chuckled. "What did he say?"

"He said there was only ever one woman he'd loved. One woman in Brighton, someone he'd known as a lad." Lucy squinted into the distance and pressed the letter to her chest. "He told me she married. I assumed she'd broken his heart."

"Lucy." A note of warning sounded in Derek's deep voice. He stopped his pacing near her chair and dipped his head to meet her gaze. "Don't you dare even think about it."

"Think about what?" Lucy stuck her nose in the air and blinked at him innocently. Several times.

"You know precisely what you're thinking about," Derek replied. "Regardless, it doesn't matter. I'm certain this cannot be the same young woman I knew in Brighton. Perhaps it's a niece who's named after her."

"Perhaps." But Lucy was already pulling out a blank sheet of vellum to write back to Mrs. Griggs's employment office.

Hughes, the butler, entered the room and cleared his throat. "Your grace," he said to Derek, "you have a visitor. Lord Swifdon has arrived."

"Ah, yes," Derek replied. "Show Julian to my study. I'll be there momentarily."

The butler bowed and left the room.

"I'm going to visit with Julian now, Lucy," Derek said firmly as he started for the door. "Please promise me you're not going to employ a governess for the care of our *children* because you think she may have known Collin in the past."

Lucy dipped her quill into the inkpot that sat on the far side of her desk. "I don't intend to do anything of the sort."

"Good." Derek paused at the threshold. "I'll help you look at the rest of the letters later."

"Thank you, darling," Lucy said, already bent over the vellum, scribbling.

Derek flashed her one last, doubtful look as he strode from the room, and a satisfied smile immediately spread across Lucy's face in his wake. She had no intention of hiring the woman based on the woman's past relationship with Collin, but it certainly couldn't hurt to find out if she was the same young woman in question, could it?

Lucy bent back over her paper and wrote a short missive to Mrs. Griggs, asking the woman to arrange an interview three days hence with one Miss Erienne Stone, formerly of Brighton.

CHAPTER TWO

Collin Hunt crossed his arms over his chest and glared at his commanding officer, Lord Treadway. "You're forcing me to leave?"

"I'm forcing you to go on holiday. I don't care what you do for the next fortnight, but you won't be working." Treadway reared back in his seat and gave Collin a hard look. "You've been at it nonstop without so much as a day off for years now. It's time you had a break, Hunt."

Collin smoothed a hand down the front of his woolen uniform. He paced away, then turned to frown at Treadway. "Is it because I snapped at Cooper?"

"Cooper, Martin, and Atwell by my count." Treadway arched a brow. "Not to mention the incident with Lord Benning last week."

Collin clenched a fist. "Damn it, Treadway, you know why—"

"He was wrong. I'm well aware of it. I agree with you, but you must admit the way you handled it left something to be desired. You need a break, Hunt. And that is an order."

"I don't want a break." The declaration came out of Collin's mouth through clenched teeth.

"I don't care," came Treadway's droll reply. "Now leave my office and this building. I don't want to see you again until after the first of September."

"As you wish, sir." Ever the soldier, Collin clicked his heels together, saluted his commanding officer, pivoted sharply, and marched out of the office. He turned right toward his own office instead of left toward the building's exit.

"Hunt!" came Treadway's voice from behind his desk, as though the man could see through the walls. He knew Collin too well. "Do not stop at your office and get paperwork. Leave. Now!"

Damn it. Collin turned once again and marched past Treadway's open door in the opposite direction, refusing to spare the man another glance.

Jamming his hands in the pockets of his coat, Collin left the building and walked toward St. James, where his apartments were located. For once, he strode with his head down, staring at the sidewalk, lost in thought. A bloody fortnight? Without working? He'd never be able to stand it. He'd been serving his majesty in the royal army since he was a lad of sixteen. He'd fought in the wars, rescued prisoners, and foiled plots against the government while working as a spy. Now he was a general assigned to the Home Office. And while the paperwork he was forced to do these days was not nearly as exciting as his time on the Continent, fighting Napoleon's best, he still felt as if he was making a difference, protecting and defending his country. Something his family had essentially dedicated their lives to. Even Adam used his printing press to further the cause of the military and recruit new soldiers.

Collin scrubbed a palm against the back of his neck and

kicked at a stone in the dusty roadway. A fortnight without working? Was that possible? Who was he without his work? More importantly, what in the bloody hell was he supposed to *do*? He could go to Brighton and visit his mother. She would like that.

But Brighton brought back memories he didn't relish, and he could only be in his mother's company for so long. She tended to talk incessantly and ask him repeatedly when he meant to settle down and produce grandchildren. It didn't matter that his brother Derek already had two children, Mary and Ralph, while Adam had two sons, Frederick and Allan. Mothers had a habit of wanting grandchildren from *all* of their offspring.

Collin was already in a foul mood. Visiting Mother and being nagged wouldn't help his disposition. No, he had to find something else to do. *A holiday*, Treadway had said. What, take the waters in Bath? Collin would be bored stiff. Travel to Dover and take a packet to Calais? He'd seen plenty of France during the wars, thank you very much.

There was only one thing he could think to do. Only one thing that wouldn't drive him completely mad. His brother Derek, the duke, usually retired to his country estate this time of year. The house was large and comfortable. Collin adored his niece and nephew, and was quite fond of his sprightly sister-in-law, Lucy. He appreciated his older brother's company and wise counsel. Besides, Derek was always up for talking about politics. At least Collin would be able to enjoy that, even if he couldn't do actual work.

Turning onto St. James Street, he made his way to the building that led up to his second-floor apartments, opened the door, and jogged up the stairs. He pulled his key from his inside coat pocket and blew out a deep breath. Fine. He had little choice. He would take a bloody holiday, at Derek's country house.

CHAPTER THREE

Erienne Stone smoothed a hand over her middle, took a deep breath, and lifted her other gloved fist to employ the brass knocker that rested on the front door of The Duke of Claringdon's town house.

She hadn't expected to be chosen for an interview for this particular position, and now that she was here, staring at the black-lacquered entrance of the imposing town house, her insides were a mass of nerves. She briefly considered turning and hurrying all the way back to Mrs. Griggs's offices.

Mrs. Griggs was a nice, efficient woman, and she'd promised Erienne she would help her find suitable work as a governess, but Erienne had no clue the lady would submit her credentials to the illustrious Duke of Claringdon's household.

Erienne's last place of employment had been in Shropsbury, taking care of two darling children for Baron Hilltop, a friend of her father's. It had been a lovely time, the last fourteen years, but the children had grown up, as children tend to do. Lady Hilltop had tried to assist Erienne in finding a new position, but there hadn't been anyone in the area in need of a governess.

Finally, Lady Hilltop had helped Erienne pack her small trunk for London and had given her an excellent reference to present to Mrs. Griggs. Mrs. Griggs owned an employment office in town, and Lady Hilltop's friends had recommended the woman's services. Erienne had taken off in a midday mail coach to London. That had been barely a sennight ago, and now here she was, going for her first interview at the town house of none other than the renowned Duke of Claringdon.

She might not have been so nervous if she didn't *know* the Duke of Claringdon. Or, more correctly, had known him in her youth. But she doubted very much if Mrs. Griggs would believe her if she'd said to the lady, "I cannot possibly interview with the Duke of Claringdon because I was once madly in love with his brother." It sounded insane even to her own ears, and she knew it was true. Besides, even if Mrs. Griggs did believe her, the woman might just question Erienne's sanity for allowing a duke's brother to slip through her fingers.

At any rate, that had all been an age ago, and Erienne needed work. She wasn't about to mark herself as particular and troublesome by refusing her first interview. Besides, she highly doubted the illustrious Duke of Claringdon, the war-hero duke, the Duke of Decisive, as he'd come to be called, would even remember a young lady from Brighton who'd been in the company of his brother Collin a time or two. It was presumptuous of Erienne to think the duke would remember her name or her face, especially if she arrived on his doorstep in an attempt to gain employment from him. Besides, the lady of the house, the duchess, would most likely be the one interviewing a governess for her children. Erienne had little to worry about.

So why was her stomach tied in knots as she waited for the front door to open?

When it did, a distinguished-looking butler stood there, staring down his nose at her. Baron Hilltop's home had been small and far less imposing. The servants had all been friendly and relaxed compared to what she'd heard about the servants in the houses of the upper crust in London. Why, precisely, had she thought it was a good idea to come to London again?

"Yes?" the butler intoned, staring at her as if she were a chimney sweep with a sooty nose.

"I …" She swallowed the lump in her throat and tried again. "I'm here to see the Duch…ess of Claringdon, her grace. I have an appointment," she hastened to add.

"Your name?"

Drat. Of course she should have given her name first. She has was a complete ninny. "Miss Er…Erienne Stone."

The butler blinked at her slowly, his face registering neither recognition of the name nor the intention to send her packing. Servants at the finest households were apparently trained to show no emotion whatsoever. She'd do well to remember that for her next interview, because she had no intention of actually securing this particular position. Even if she were offered it, she'd be a fool to take it. She'd come here to please Mrs. Griggs, to gain some practice in the art of the interview, and because the sum of money Mrs. Griggs mentioned as the pay for being the governess in the house of a duke and a duchess was an amount that would more than pay for Peter's surgery.

And very well … If she was being *completely* honest, she'd also come to see if there was any possibility whatsoever of learning the slightest piece of news about … Collin.

The thought had stolen the breath from her lungs, but she couldn't help herself. She simply couldn't. It was wrong and

11

it was madness, but she hadn't been able to keep herself from coming here today. The papers often held news about the duke and his dashing wife, but she'd found little about Collin over the years. She couldn't help her curiosity. Not because she still cared for him. Never that. Their involvement with each other had been a lifetime ago. But merely because she … wondered about him from time to time. Was he happy? Was he married? Did he have a son with his own dark hair and green eyes?

The butler stood to the side and opened the door wider, scattering Erienne's thoughts. "Come in. Her grace is expecting you, Miss Stone."

Erienne nearly doubled over with relief. She stepped inside the grand marble-lined foyer and tried not to gawk at the exquisite room. A double staircase made entirely of marble and sleek, polished wood snaked its way up on either side of the cavernous space. White, shining marble floors spread in front of her as far as the eye could see. Highly polished wood tables sat on either side of the room with elaborate golden candelabras gracing the centers of both. The place smelled like lemon and costly wax, and a huge crystal chandelier hung from the ceiling between the two sides of the staircase.

The interior was sparse, but gorgeous and tasteful, a far cry from the tiny cottage at the end of the lane where Derek Hunt and his two brothers had grown up in Brighton. She'd always known the Hunt brothers were special, but Derek's success made tears sting her eyes. She quickly blinked them away.

Aware of her gawking, Erienne snapped her mouth shut. She wasn't certain she was dressed well enough to *enter* this house, let alone apply for employment within its magnificent walls. She *was* certain the butler's livery cost more than the entire fourteen years of pay she'd received while working for the Hilltop family. She clutched at her simple white cotton reticule and glanced down at her serviceable white cotton gown and light green woolen pelisse. Her kid slippers were also white and also serviceable, but just last week she'd added small satin ribbons to the tops to make them more stylish. Now she'd never been more relieved that she'd taken the time to do something so frivolous.

"May I take your coat and gloves?" Not meeting her gaze, the butler held out one stiff arm for the articles.

Erienne hurriedly removed both items and handed them to the man, who set them neatly aside before saying, "This way." He walked like a statue come to life toward two large wooden doors attached to the foyer.

Erienne scrambled behind him to keep up with his long strides, gulping and hoping he hadn't heard the unattractive noise. No doubt servants in so fine a house didn't do such vulgar things as gulp. There had been little to gulp about at the Hilltops' house.

The butler knocked once before pushing open the doors and stepping inside. Erienne followed him and tried not to stare at the gorgeous lady perched on the settee in the center of the room. The woman had curly, black hair that was pinned atop her head. She wore a lovely emerald green gown and a smile brightened her pretty features.

"Your grace," the butler intoned. "May I present Miss Stone?"

To Erienne's amazement, the lady stood, hurried over to her, and grasped her hands as if they were reuniting friends. "Miss Stone, I've been expecting you. Please, come and sit with me."

Erienne had no choice but to follow the woman back toward the settee.

"Please do bring tea, Hughes," the duchess said.

The butler nodded, bowed, and took his leave.

The duchess resumed her seat and patted the space next to her to indicate that Erienne should sit there. Erienne lowered herself as gracefully as possible to the settee and blinked at the duchess. Did great ladies stand and greet potential governesses in such a friendly fashion?

Apparently this one did, but it was entirely unexpected. And to have tea ordered as if they were friends sitting down to gossip? Quite unexpected indeed. Erienne had heard the Duchess of Claringdon was beautiful and lively, but she hadn't quite expected…this. The lady was beautiful, however. That much was true. Even more so up close. She had two different-colored eyes, one hazel, one blue, and her smile was both friendly and mischievous.

Erienne folded her sweating hands in her lap and watched the pretty duchess carefully.

The grand lady's next words surprised her. "How old are you, Miss Stone?"

"Pardon?" Surely she'd heard the woman incorrectly.

"I do hope you don't think I'm being rude," the duchess continued, "but I wondered if you were near my husband's age."

Apprehension skittered along Erienne's spine. "I turned two and thirty this year, your grace."

The duchess tapped a manicured finger against her cheek and narrowed her eyes as if deep in thought. "And you come from Brighton, correct? That's what your letter of recommendation said."

"Most recently, I came from Shropsbury," Erienne replied. Brighton? Had Mrs. Griggs mentioned Brighton?

The duchess frowned. "Have you ever been married?"

Erienne furrowed her brow. These weren't precisely the questions she'd expected when she'd accepted this interview. What did her birthplace or potential marital status have to do with being a governess? "I'm highly qualified, your grace. I

14

spent the last fourteen years with Baron and Lady Hilltop. They wrote me a lovely letter of recommendation. Would you care to see it?"

"Yes. Of course I believe you're highly qualified as a governess, Miss Stone. It's just that..."

The butler interrupted the duchess when he stepped into the room with the tea tray. While he went about setting it on the little table and arranging everything just so, Erienne shifted uncomfortably in her seat. Oddly, the duchess never once took her unusual gaze from Erienne's face, as though the woman found her like some kind of compelling puzzle to be turned this way and that.

"Tea?" the duchess finally asked Erienne, mercifully turning her attention to the tray.

Erienne had never been served tea by a duchess before, but she felt it might be rude to refuse it after the woman had gone to the trouble of having it delivered. "Yes, please?" It emerged as more of a question than a request.

Perhaps fine London households did this sort of thing. Erienne's friend Rebecca, who worked as Lady Hilltop's personal maid, had worked in London previously. But Rebecca hadn't mentioned any of these things. Now that Erienne considered it, however, Rebecca had worked for a viscountess. Perhaps a duchess did things like serve tea to servants. It all seemed quite odd and uncomfortable, however.

The duchess poured Erienne a cup of tea. "Sugar?" she asked.

"Yes, please, one lump."

"Only one?" The other woman's eyes widened. She dropped the requested lump into the cup and handed it to Erienne before pouring her own cup and proceeding to drop an inordinate amount of sugar lumps into it. "I adore sugar in my tea," she explained with a laugh.

"I see that," Erienne replied, raising her brows. Drat. She could kick herself for such an uninteresting reply.

"Now what was I saying?" The duchess lifted her teacup to her lips and took a sip. "Oh, yes, I asked if you'd ever been married. Have you?"

Erienne took a deep breath. Clearly the woman was interested in her past. Very well. Perhaps it stood to reason. Someone as grand as the duchess wouldn't want to find out later that the governess she'd employed to raise her children had some sort of sordid history.

"I have not," she replied quietly. *I came close once. And I desperately wanted to.* She shook her head. Where had *those* thoughts come from? She hadn't entertained them in years. Being around someone who no doubt knew Collin had possibly served to dredge up bad memories.

Suddenly, a wild impulse to bolt for the door seized her. She glanced in its direction and forced herself to swallow another sip from her cup. She shouldn't have come here. She needed to get this over with as quickly as possible, thank the duchess for her valuable time, and leave. There had to be a more suitable, less imposing position with a nice viscount or someone else available. She would ask Mrs. Griggs to send her on a more reasonable interview next time.

"Hmm. But you are from Brighton originally, are you not?" the duchess continued.

This was excruciating. "I was born there. Yes." Erienne concentrated on taking tiny, ladylike sips of tea, one after the other.

The duchess narrowed her eyes on Erienne. "Do you know my husband? He was merely Derek Hunt when he lived in Brighton, of course."

Erienne's teacup instantly commenced a noisy rattle in its saucer, and she quickly set it on the little table and folded her trembling hands in her lap. How should she reply? Was it a coincidence that the duchess was asking whether she'd known Derek in Brighton? Derek couldn't possibly have seen her name and remembered *her*, could he? Blast Mrs. Griggs for even mentioning her relationship to Brighton. Regardless, Erienne had no intention of lying to the pretty duchess. What would be the point?

"I do remember Derek Hunt." She glanced away, out the window. "And his brothers." She swallowed hard. That admission had been more difficult than she'd expected.

"Collin?" the duchess added, her voice almost breathless. "You remember Collin, don't you?" When Erienne looked at her again, the woman's eyes searched Erienne's face intently, with what she could only describe as ... hope?

This was worse than excruciating. It was torturous. Erienne took a deep breath and pressed a hand against her middle, which was lurching in consternation. Hopefully she could make it to the street corner before casting up her accounts. It had been a hideous idea to come here.

"Your grace, I'm not entirely certain I would be the best person for this position." She tried to stand, but the duchess reached out, placed a hand on Erienne's arm, and softly squeezed. "No, please stay. I didn't mean to make you uncomfortable, Miss Stone."

Her heart thumping in her chest, Erienne forced herself to sit again. She bit the inside of her cheek and prayed for the dignity to remain calm. How had the Duchess of Claringdon heard of her? How had the grand lady learned of her past with Collin? None of it made any sense. Surely she was in a dream and would wake any moment, back at her small bedchamber at Baron Hilltop's estate, the birds chirping in the tree outside her window.

The duchess set her teacup aside and pulled a sheet of vellum from the table in front of her. She eyed it up and down and then turned back to Erienne. "You come highly recommended. According to Mrs. Griggs, your previous employment was with a boy and a girl in Shropsbury."

Erienne expelled a sigh of relief. She could breathe again now that the interview was more customary. "Yes, Timothy and Evelyn. They were lovely children. I adored them."

"I have a boy and a girl myself," the duchess said. "Mary can be a handful at times. But I daresay even at barely two years old, Ralph is nearly as charming as his father."

Erienne smiled at that. "Mary and Ralph. Those are lovely names."

A smile lit the duchess's unusually colored eyes. "Yes, we named them after my beloved aunt, and my brother who died in childhood."

"I'm sorry to hear that," Erienne replied, glancing down at her slippers. She knew what it was like to grieve for a sibling. Peter might still be alive, but his injuries had taken his speech and movement.

"Do you have any brothers or sisters, Miss Stone?"

Erienne lifted her head again to meet the duchess's watchful gaze. "I have one brother. He was gravely injured in the war."

"Oh no. I'm quite sorry," the duchess replied, her voice softening. "So many fine men were hurt or killed in the wars. Derek knew so many of them."

Erienne nodded solemnly. She picked up her teacup again and dared to take a sip. She should keep the conversation on topic. The duchess didn't want to hear about Peter's war injuries. "I've never worked in so fine a household as this, your grace. I'm not entirely certain I'd be qualified to—"

"That doesn't matter to me in the least," the duchess replied. "I quite liked what you said in your letter about being kind but also strict. Mary needs that."

Erienne nodded. "Yes, well, I'm certain you've received many, many letters from far more qualified ladies than me."

"The stack of letters was nearly a foot high," the duchess admitted with a half-smile.

The teacup nearly toppled out of Erienne's hand. "Are you quite serious?"

"Entirely." The duchess sighed. "I still haven't gone through all of them."

Erienne settled her shoulders. "I hope this doesn't seem ill-mannered of me, your grace, but why in heaven's name did you pick *me* to interview if you have that many applicants for the position?"

The duchess pushed a dark curl behind one ear and took another sip of her heavily sugared tea, failing utterly to hide her sly smile behind the dainty cup. "Because you, Miss Stone, were the only applicant who my brother-in-law apparently used to be in love with."

CHAPTER FOUR

T he traveling chaise had barely left Collin near the front steps of Huntingdon, his brother's country estate, when two footmen rushed out to gather his trunk. Derek came striding out of the house behind them. He stopped next to Collin and clapped him on the back. "I thought you wouldn't be here until tomorrow, Coll."

"Yes, my apologies for the early arrival. I'd intended to spend one more day in London, finishing some paperwork, but Treadway found me in my office and took the bloody paperwork away. I had to sneak around like a bloody spy."

Derek threw back his head and laughed. "You are a spy, and apparently not a very good one any longer if you couldn't elude Treadway."

"I'd no idea he would hunt me down like a criminal," Collin grumbled.

Derek laughed again. "That sounds like Treadway. Not to worry about coming early, though. We've only just arrived this morning ourselves. Come into the study and have a drink."

The footmen scurried off with Collin's trunk, and Derek

led the way into the house. They walked through the fine foyer and down a marble corridor to the dark wooden doors of the study. The grand house smelled of lemon and turpentine. Obviously the servants had been hard at work preparing it for their master's arrival.

As soon as they entered the study, Derek immediately went to the sideboard and poured two glasses of brandy. He handed one to Collin before he took a seat behind the large mahogany desk that graced the center of the room. Collin accepted the glass and wandered to the window. He braced a shoulder against the wall, crossed his booted feet at the ankles, and stared off across the meadow toward the lake at the back of the property. God, it felt good to be in the country. Some of his resentment toward Treadway eased a little, try as Collin might to cling to it.

"Come for some relaxation, did you?" Derek asked, settling back into his large, leather chair.

Collin sighed and rubbed a hand through his hair. "I had no choice." He took a sip of brandy.

"What precisely did Treadway say to you?"

A grim smile played across Collin's face as he glanced at his brother. "He told me I could do anything I wanted for the next fortnight, as long as it's not work."

"Then he caught you working?" Derek asked with a grin.

Collin lowered his brows. "It's bloody ridiculous to force someone to take a holiday."

Derek tilted his head to the side and regarded his brother. "It might do you some good, you know."

Collin rolled his eyes. "Don't you start, too."

Derek contemplated the brown liquid in his glass. "I'm merely saying relaxation isn't terrible."

"It's also not what it's cracked up to be." Collin took another drink, and this time it burned down his throat and settled hotly in his gut.

"I'm pleased you decided to pay us a visit at least. We'll enjoy ourselves. Go shooting, riding, have a few dinners with the local gentry. Drink." Derek lifted his glass with a smile.

Collin leaned his head against the window frame and sighed. "Yes, well, I decided if I must spend time away from work, I might as well pay my niece and nephew a visit." He glanced toward the door. "Where's Lucy, by the by?"

"Seeing to the children," Derek replied. "She just hired a new governess, and she's been busy showing the woman how she likes the nursery to be managed."

Collin turned his head to look at his brother. "What happened to the other governess? Miss Langley, was it?"

Derek cracked a smile. "She married."

"Thank heavens," Collin replied. "She was a lovely young woman, but I got the distinct impression that Lucy was trying to match me with her. It made me deuced uncomfortable."

Derek laughed. "You weren't wrong. Lucy adores matchmaking, as I'm certain you've gathered. She tried to match poor Miss Langley with half the male guests who entered the house before Mr. Benton came along."

Collin stared out the window again. "I wish them well."

"I do too. I just hope Lucy doesn't try to matchmake the new governess."

Collin moved from the window and dropped into one of the two large leather chairs that faced Derek's desk. He arranged his jacket. He'd discarded his uniform for regular clothing, garments he rarely wore. He felt odd in them. "Is she comely?"

Derek took another sip of brandy. "Honestly, I don't know. I haven't met her yet. Lucy hired her just before we left London and provided her with fare to take the mail coach here. The woman arrived this morning, not an hour after we did, and Lucy hurried her off to the children's rooms before I had a chance to greet her."

"Well, the poor woman should be careful. If she doesn't want to marry, Lucy may not be the best choice of employer for her," Collin said with a laugh.

"I've tried to explain to Lucy a half-dozen times that it's not particularly conducive to keeping a governess for the children if she continues to marry them off one by one." Derek sighed. "But Lucy cannot seem to help herself. She's says she's a matchmaker at heart."

Collin knocked back the rest of his drink. "As long as she doesn't try to matchmake me, I'm fine with it."

"I'll be certain to remind her to leave you be," Derek said. "Now, what's on the agenda for the next fortnight?"

Collin sighed and stretched out his legs in front of him, staring glumly at the reflection of sunlight on his polished boots. "I suppose I should see about relaxing. To that end, I intend to have a completely peaceful stay in the country with absolutely nothing to worry me."

Derek lifted his glass. "I'll drink to that."

CHAPTER FIVE

E rienne glanced around the magnificent bedchamber that belonged to Lady Mary Hunt, the duchess's adorable, precocious, three-year-old daughter. The child was as beautiful as her mother. She had the duchess's curly black hair and her father's dark eyes. Lady Mary had already endeared herself to Erienne by toddling over, executing a perfect little curtsy, and saying, "It's vewwy nice to meet you, Miss Stwone."

Erienne and Lucy had exchanged glances and hid their smiles while Erienne performed a similar curtsy to little Lady Mary. "My pleasure, Lady Mary. And may I say you have fine manners, indeed."

"Thwank you," Lady Mary replied. She clasped her little hands together and asked, "Do you have a dwog?"

"A dwo—?" Frowning, Erienne glanced at Lucy for an interpretation.

Lucy smiled and shook her head. "She wants a dog. She's been asking for one for as long as she could speak."

"Oh," Erienne said, lifting her skirts and crouching so that she was at Lady Mary's eye level. "I do not have a dog, but I should very much like one. I adore them."

Lady Mary clapped her hands. "Oh, gwood," the little girl exclaimed. "I want to name my dwog Cinderwella."

Erienne pressed her lips together to keep from laughing. She could tell the little girl took the subject of procuring a dog and naming it quite seriously. "Cinderella?"

"I gave her that book for her birthday. She adores it," Lucy explained.

Erienne turned her attention back to Lady Mary. "Well, I think Ella is a perfectly lovely name for a dog."

"Me twoo," Lady Mary said, beaming.

Lucy placed a hand on her daughter's shoulder. "Go play with Ralph and Anna in the corner, darling," she said, pointing toward where her son and a nursemaid sat across the room near a stack of wooden blocks. Ralph was sitting up straight, shaking one of the blocks in his little fist. Mary happily scampered off to join them.

"Anna will be your assistant," Lucy continued to Erienne, nodding toward the young maid. "She's been the children's nursemaid since they were born."

Erienne blinked. "Assistant?"

"Yes." Lucy waved a hand in the air. "You know, for when you need a few moments of peace. Or help with lessons. You'll also have a maid who serves your meals and theirs, and another maid who does your laundry and theirs, and one who cleans your rooms and—"

"I'm not accustomed to having help." Erienne had never even heard of such a thing. At Hilltop House, she and the other upper servants had been served meals by the under servants, but that had been the extent of any help she'd received in her position. She'd certainly never had a nurse-maid to help watch the children, or a maid to clean her room

25

or do her laundry. She'd been responsible for bringing her own laundry down to the laundry maids each week.

"I understand," Lucy replied. "But I think it's best if you're able to concentrate on the children's studies. I want both of them to begin learning French right away."

"Of course." Erienne wasn't about to argue with a duchess over the extravagance of her household. Besides, it stood to reason that in such a fine home there would be more servants. But it was yet another reason she was still not entirely certain why she'd accepted this position. Would she ever feel comfortable here?

"They're darling children," Erienne said. "And I've never seen such fine bedchambers." She gestured around the cavernous space that was Lady Mary's room.

Lucy threaded her arm through Erienne's. "Now, let me show you your rooms."

"Rooms?" Erienne echoed. She'd assumed she would have one room, no doubt a lovely one, but at Hilltop House, her accommodations had been limited to a single serviceable bedchamber.

"Anna, we'll be back soon," Lucy called to the nursemaid, who nodded and continued her play with the children.

They left Mary's nursery and strolled down the hall, past Ralph's equally large bedchamber to the end of the corridor, where Lucy pushed open a wide door to reveal a room that stole Erienne's breath.

"This is your bedchamber," Lucy said, sweeping her hand in front of her as she showed Erienne the huge, elegantly appointed space. The room was much grander than the one she'd had at the Hilltops' residence, decorated in hues of green and lavender. Her bed was a large, fancy thing with a white satin tent over it, a new down mattress, matching fluffy pillows and the finest white linens she'd ever touched. Fresh flowers and wax candles (no tallow) rested on the bedside table. Erienne wanted to pinch herself with glee.

Lucy pointed. "Through that door is the sitting room, and over there is the dressing room."

"Dressing room? I have my own dressing room?" Erienne couldn't help herself. She lifted her skirts and hurried through the first door. The dressing room had its own dressing table with a small lavender tufted stool sitting in front of it. The top of the table was filled with pots and bottles, a silver-handled brush and a matching mirror. There was a large cheval looking glass in the corner, and a wardrobe nearly double the size of the one she'd been given at Hilltop House.

Keeping her lips tightly pressed together to hide her amazement, Erienne turned and made her way back through the bedchamber to the sitting room. Lucy followed her, watching with a faint smile.

The sitting room was a cozy space with an obviously expensive fitted carpet, and (oh, goodness!) she had her own *fireplace* in this room too, for heaven's sake. A comfortable-looking chair with a footstool sat next to the fireplace with a small table beside it. The walls were lined with whitewashed bookcases of all wonderfully welcomed things. A plethora of books graced the shelves. There was a cream-colored quilt splayed across the chair, and two fluffy fur-lined slippers sat in front of the footstool. A silver-plated tea service perched on the footstool, completing the perfectly relaxing little space.

Erienne turned to face Lucy and couldn't help the wonder that no doubt shined in her eyes. She pressed her palms to both cheeks. "These rooms are beyond magnificent, your grace. I couldn't possibly—"

"Ah, ah, ah." Lucy wagged a finger at her. "I've already told you, you must call me Lucy. We don't stand on formality with our trusted servants in this house. And don't you dare refuse these rooms. They're meant for you. And well-deserved. You'll need time for yourself after spending so much of it with the children."

Erienne expelled her breath. "I was going to say, I couldn't possibly ask for more."

"Excellent," Lucy replied with a sparkling smile. "I'm so happy you're pleased."

Erienne made her way back into the bedchamber. She hadn't noticed it at first, but on the far wall there was a lovely painting of two little girls playing in a bright, flowered field. Looking at it, her heart swelled. She'd always wanted a sister, and her fondest dream had been to have two daughters. But that was a long time ago, back when she had allowed herself to do things like dream of marriage and children of her own.

She shook her head. It did no good to contemplate the past. She must look to the future. Hadn't that been her maxim since the day she'd left Brighton behind, wiping away the last of her tears and refusing to ever shed them again for any man?

Least of all, Collin Hunt.

"I'll just leave you to look around for a bit," Lucy said. "I'll meet you back in the nursery when you're ready."

Erienne nodded happily and glanced around. She wouldn't take long, but she dearly appreciated the few minutes to explore her new home. She had been apprehensive agreeing to this position. In the last few days since first meeting with Lucy, she'd refused it outright more than once. But the duchess refused to take no for an answer. It wasn't until Lucy mentioned a sum of money that Erienne had seldom dreamed of that she finally relented and told the duchess she would *think* about it. After all, the amount Lucy had offered for one month's pay had been more than she'd made in an entire year at the Hilltops'.

Erienne would be a complete fool to refuse it. Her brother needed surgery to remove a bullet from his back and she was used to sending all her money home. She couldn't pass up the opportunity to pay for all of Peter's medical bills, and then some, over the fact that she might encounter a man from her past if she took the position. That would have been entirely selfish of her. She had been merely thinking about it, however, not at all convinced that she would take the position, but she'd discovered to her acute chagrin that Lucy Hunt could be extremely convincing, almost ridiculously so, when she wanted to be. She'd sent Erienne letters every day begging her to accept, along with gifts of gowns, flowers, and books. She'd even written to Lady Hilltop and asked her to put in a good word for her.

The lady had written posthaste to tell Erienne she'd lost her wits if she refused a position in the illustrious Duchess of Claringdon's household. "Why, I daresay the entirety of Hilltop House could fit in one bedchamber at Huntingdon."

But now that she was actually here, Erienne's middle was filled with nerves at the prospect of seeing Derek. Had Lucy told him about her? He had to remember her. How else had Lucy known who she was?

Erienne didn't hold out much hope (fear?) of seeing Collin. Lucy had assured her that he worked constantly and stayed in his apartments in London. He could usually be found in his offices at Whitehall, neither of which were places Erienne would ever be likely to visit in her role as governess to the duke and duchess's children. She supposed she might face him eventually at some holiday like Christmastide, but that was a long way off.

Erienne trailed her way over to stand in front of the painting of the two girls. She'd admitted her past with Collin to Lucy, but had significantly downplayed the effect it had had on her, though she had asked Lucy to promise not to attempt to arrange for them to meet. "I realize it may come to pass, eventually, but I would dislike it immensely if you were to … orchestrate it." She'd cleared her throat, hoping the duchess wouldn't ask too many personal questions about her past with Collin.

"I completely understand," Lucy had replied, patting her on the shoulder and giving her a sympathetic look that Erienne greatly appreciated.

That had been the end of their discussion about Collin, thank heavens.

Now, Erienne twirled in a circle, taking in the gorgeous surroundings once more. The children seemed well-behaved, the pay was exorbitant, and her suite was magnificent. She might have an awkward moment with Derek at first, and someday she might have to suffer through an excruciating encounter with Collin, but she would worry about that when the time came. For now, she intended to enjoy every moment of this glorious new position.

Lucy had been beyond generous in allowing her a few moments to settle in. She should get back. She mustn't take advantage of the duchess's generosity. Erienne hurried into the corridor, closing the door to her rooms behind her, and made her way back to the nursery.

When she entered the room she stopped short, her breath caught in her throat.

Collin was standing there.

Erienne's heart pounded so heavily her chest hurt. The tall, dark-haired man faced away from her, his broad shoulders blocking Lucy from her view, but she could hear the duchess's voice coming from the other side of him. Wait. No. It wasn't Collin. She closed her eyes and expelled her pent-up breath. It was Derek. Of course it was Derek, not Collin, standing there. The two brothers simply looked so much alike. She took a fortifying gulp of air for good measure and straightened her shoulders.

"Your grace?" she called softly.

Lucy stepped around her large husband, a wide smile on her face, as Derek turned to Erienne.

"Ah, here she is now. I was just telling Derek about you," Lucy said.

Erienne lowered her chin, but forced herself to meet Derek's eyes, which instantly widened. The last time she'd seen him, he'd been perhaps seventeen years old. On leave from the army, he'd come home to visit his family. He'd been a tall, handsome young man, and now he was larger and even more handsome. Except for his dark eyes, he looked so much like Collin.

Her knees nearly buckled. Why had she done this to herself? Was the money and the suite of rooms truly worth this constant reminder of Collin? She pressed her lips together. Hard.

Lucy hurried over to her side and threaded her arm through Erienne's as she'd done so many times before. "Derek, may I present Miss—"

"Stone," Derek finished, his dark gaze narrowed on her. His face was completely devoid of emotion, but his nostrils flared.

Erienne concentrated on controlling her erratic breathing. She'd no idea if Lucy had told Derek that she'd hired a governess from Brighton whom he'd once known. Likely the duchess had, given the fact that Lucy had already known what Collin once meant to Erienne. Where else would Lucy have learned about her past with Collin if not from Derek?

But Erienne had also assumed that Derek had agreed with Lucy's decision to hire her, or she would not be here. Now, looking at the obvious frown on the duke's face, Erienne realized she'd made a grave mistake. She should not have assumed Lucy told her husband she'd hired the girl who used to love Collin. Drat. Drat. Drat. This was dreadfully awkward.

"Good afternoon, your grace," Erienne said belatedly, dropping into her most formal curtsy.

A muscle ticked in Derek's jaw. "Miss Stone," he intoned. "Lovely to see you again. It's been, ahem, many years." He clasped his hands behind his ramrod-straight back. It was obvious the man had spent many years in battle. He commanded attention even simply addressing his new governess.

Erienne had to squelch the urge to hide behind Lucy. "Many, many years," Erienne echoed, wishing the floor would open up and swallow her.

Anna, the nursemaid, was doing a fine job keeping the children occupied in the corner, so Erienne couldn't even use that as an excuse to run off and perform her duties. Instead, she stood there, still as a statue while Derek turned to his wife and said in a tone clearly laced with anger, "Lucy, may I have a word with you? *Privately.*"

CHAPTER SIX

Lucy patted Erienne's shoulder and gave her an encouraging smile before following Derek out of Mary's bedchamber. They walked down the corridor and around the corner where they wouldn't be overheard by the two servants or the children.

The muscle continued to tick in Derek's jaw when he turned to her and said, "You promised me you wouldn't choose a governess based on her past relationship with Collin."

Lucy nodded. "And I didn't. I met with Miss Stone and spoke to her former employer, as well as the woman who recommended her from the employment office. Miss Stone is highly qualified. She speaks fluent French and—"

"Lucy," Derek's voice was low and agitated, a tone she didn't often hear him use. "You promised—"

She folded her arms over her chest. "I never promised not to *hire* Miss Stone. I only promised not to hire Miss Stone *only* because of her connection with Collin. And I assure you, I have not." She ended her sentence with a firm nod.

Derek scrubbed a hand through his hair and blew out an

obviously frustrated breath. "But you *are* intending to play matchmaker with Miss Stone and Collin, aren't you?"

Lucy lifted one shoulder in a shrug. "If it ever comes to pass that they see each other, I cannot help it if the two of them still have unresolved feelings for each other."

Derek narrowed his eyes. "What do you mean, if it ever comes to pass? Of course it will come to pass."

Lucy pushed a curl behind her ear and affected a thoughtful expression. "It's true. Miss Stone *was* concerned about the possibility of encountering Collin, of course, but I assured her that we rarely see him."

Derek cursed under his breath and strode toward a nearby window, where he looked out across the meadow. "Damn it, Lucy. Collin is here."

Her eyes went round as saucers. "What?"

Derek gave one curt nod. "He arrived this morning. He wrote me a letter not a sennight ago telling me Treadway had ordered him on holiday. He's here for the next fortnight."

Lucy pressed her lips together to keep from smiling and tilted her nose in the air. "Well, you cannot blame me for orchestrating this, as you somehow saw fit to not inform me that Collin was coming."

Derek pounded the side of his fist against the wall. "Damn. Damn. Damn. It slipped my mind. Besides, I knew you'd be nothing but pleased by a visit from Collin."

"Of course I am. I adore Collin."

"Yes, but now you will use his visit to play matchmaker. I can tell. Your eyes are already sparkling with joy and mischief, not concern as they should be."

Lucy waved a hand in the air. "I cannot help how my eyes sparkle, darling. But I admit, I am pleased. Even more pleased now, to be honest." She rubbed her hands together.

"Oh, no you don't," Derek warned, his eyes narrowed on her. "You don't get your way that easily."

Lucy gave an innocent blink. "I don't see how you can blame me. I didn't invite Collin here. He came of his own accord. This has nothing to do with my machinations, even though I freely admit it's a positively delightful turn of events."

"Damn it, Lucy." Derek grimaced and turned back toward the window. "Why do these things always seem to happen when you're up to your matchmaking tricks? If you hadn't hired a governess you knew Collin had a history with, we wouldn't have to worry about the impending awkwardness."

"You're thinking of it all wrong, darling," she said with a sigh, laying her hand on his back and patting him. "The world has a way of making things happen just when they are meant to. Far be it from me to interrupt the natural order of such things."

Derek turned to face her and rubbed his jaw. "I suppose we could attempt to keep them separated while Collin is here …"

"Nonsense. Why should we do that? Clearly this was meant to be."

"Not *everything* is meant to be," he said dryly. "Some things are mistakes and should be avoided at all costs."

Lucy wrapped her arms around her husband's waist and squeezed him. "I believe you're forgetting how we met, darling. I was trying to keep you from courting my closest friend, who wanted nothing to do with you, and you were trying to convince me to leave you alone. If our courtship wasn't meant to be, I daresay Mary and Ralph wouldn't be here now."

"That's different." His stern expression softened as he gazed down at her and tucked an errant curl behind her ear. "That was … us."

"Need I remind you, then, of how Cass and Julian got together after she pretended to be a nonexistent person named Patience Bunbury?" Lucy returned his look with eyebrows raised. "Or how Jane and Garrett fell in love because we told each of them the other was already in love with them, just like Beatrice and Benedick in *Much Ado About Nothing?*" She paused and tapped her cheek, searching her mind for more ammunition. "I could go on."

"Please, don't." He held up both hands in surrender. "The fact is, however, we've no idea what happened back then with Collin and Miss Stone. What if they never wanted to see each other again? You said yourself that Miss Stone expressed concern about seeing Collin."

Lucy stepped back and gave another shrug. "There's only one way to find out what happens when their paths cross."

Derek leaned back against the wall and hung his head. "Collin's never going to believe we didn't do this purposely, you know."

"He'll be fine. He's a grown man, and you said yourself, it's been years. Besides, he's welcome to leave if he's offended by her presence."

Derek expelled a breath, and his shoulders lifted and relaxed. "Very well. But we must handle this delicately."

Lucy smoothed her skirts. "Delicately? What do you mean?"

"I mean you need to go inform Miss Stone that Collin is here, and I need to go break the news to Collin. Damn. Damn. Damn."

CHAPTER SEVEN

Collin brought his mount up short to stare across the valley toward the forest that lined Derek's property. The giant, multi-acre estate was a world away from the tiny cottage where they'd grown up in Brighton. Their father had been a military man, but he hadn't risen through the ranks. On the contrary, he'd been discharged from the army for drinking too heavily. But that hadn't stopped him from setting about working with his sons to ensure they became the finest military specimens they could be.

He'd been particularly harsh with Derek, forcing the young boy to make decisions quickly and without mercy. Once, he'd tossed Derek's prized toy sailboat and his puppy in two different directions into a fast-running stream. Derek had saved the puppy, of course, but their father's cruelty in making his sons tough knew few bounds.

He'd succeeded, of course. Derek was known as the Duke of Decisive and had been at Wellington's side, an integral part of the win at Waterloo. For his efforts, Derek had been awarded a dukedom and Huntingdon, the grand estate that Collin now surveyed.

Collin had chosen a slightly different route. He, too, had risen quickly in the ranks of the army, but he'd used his decision-making skills not in battle, but in becoming one of the War Office's most accomplished spies. He'd been essential in foiling a great many of the emperor's plots, and had been in extreme danger behind enemy lines more times than he cared to count. He'd used his intelligence and cunning to predict what the French would do next, and was awarded many medals and promoted time and again as a result of his success.

When the wars ended, Derek settled down to marry and become a father. He met Lucy soon after returning from Belgium, and it was obvious to anyone who saw the two of them together that they were a perfectly matched pair.

Collin, however, had rededicated himself to his majesty's service and continued to take on English missions on both domestic soil and abroad. Marriage hadn't been in the cards for him, and it wasn't something he allowed himself to dwell on. He'd come close to marriage only once, and it had been one of the most painful things he'd ever experienced. He had no wish to revisit those old emotions.

That did not, however, keep either his mother or his sister-in-law, Lucy, from attempting to place potential brides in his path. Over the years, Lucy had introduced him to scores of young ladies, and he'd been well aware that she'd hoped he would fall madly in love with one of them. He'd always kept them at arm's length, however. Perfectly polite, but in no way indicating he would like anything more than an acquaintance with any of them.

At least Lucy introduced him to strangers. He could easily deflect his sister-in-law's attempts at matchmaking. When he went to visit his mother, however, she would inevitably bring up ... Erienne. And if there was one subject Collin would not discuss, could *not* discuss, it was Erienne Stone.

He'd chosen to come to Derek's house instead of visiting his mother for a reason. He closed his eyes and breathed in lungfuls of clean, country air. It was probably good for him to get out of the coal-laden air of London awhile.

Mindlessly smoothing his hand over his horse's mane, he briefly considered Lucy's former attempts at matchmaking him with Miss Langley. Miss Langley had been a sweet young woman with a lovely disposition, but she, like all the other women Lucy had paraded before him, didn't have the sky blue eyes or silky blond hair of the young woman who'd haunted his dreams since he was a lad of sixteen.

He shook his head. Hopefully, Lucy wouldn't attempt to matchmake him with the new governess. No doubt the poor woman had no idea what she was getting herself into by taking a position with the Duchess of Claringdon. The *Matchmaker* of Claringdon should be Lucy's title, he thought with a wry smile.

She was a handful, his sister-in-law. She loved to ask Collin why he wasn't married yet. Why wasn't he? He'd told himself all these years it was because he was married to his work. It would be unfair, unkind even, to take a wife and leave her at home, day and night, alone, or possibly only with the children while he worked so many long hours.

But there was more to it than that, and he knew it.

The image of Erienne's face leaped to his memory. He always thought about her when his reflections turned to marriage. She'd been the only woman he'd even contemplated wedding, the only woman he'd ever wanted to marry, and he'd been forced to let her go. He'd tried to push it from his mind over the years, tried to ignore it, but times like this, bloody times like this when he didn't have his work to distract him, the memories crept back into his mind.

It didn't matter. Erienne was far from here. She was married to a viscount in Shropsbury, just as she should be. She probably had half a score of children by now. *Was she happy? Did she ever think of him?* Damn it. Of course not. A married woman wouldn't think of him, shouldn't think of him. It was ludicrous to even contemplate it.

The thunder of hooves caught his attention, and he turned to see Derek riding up behind him.

"There you are," his brother called as he pulled his horse up short next to Collin. "I didn't realize you'd ridden out this far."

"What else have I got to do?" Collin replied with a laugh.

"I'll take you around the entire perimeter sometime if you'd like, but we'd better get back to the house now. Lucy and the children want to see you."

"Of course." Collin nodded and gathered the reins in his gloved hand.

They both turned and began a canter back toward the house.

"Seems I forgot to tell Lucy you were coming," Derek said, his eyes fixed straight ahead on the path.

Collin lifted his brows. "Lucy's not upset, is she?"

"Only that she didn't have all week to look forward to your visit."

"Ah, well, I suppose I'll just pretend it was a surprise visit, then."

"Yes, well…" Derek's voice trailed off.

A sudden, odd tightness gripped Collin's stomach. "What? What is it?"

"Seems my forgetting to tell Lucy caused a problem elsewhere." Derek still hadn't met his gaze, a sure sign of some kind of guilt.

Collin's brows drew down. "What? How's that?"

Derek slowed his horse. Collin did the same.

"You know how certain things tend to...happen when Lucy is involved?" Derek asked.

Collin poked out his cheek with his tongue. "She is usually up to something, isn't she?"

"You could say that," Derek replied.

"What is it?" Collin asked, apprehension replacing his suspicion. Something was wrong. He could feel it.

At last, Derek met his eyes. "I have something I must tell you, Collin. Something I'm afraid you're not going to like."

CHAPTER EIGHT

"Collin? Hunt? Is here? In this house? Right now?" The words left Erienne's mouth in a staccato rhythm. She knew she sounded like a mad woman for the way she'd uttered them, but she couldn't help herself. The implication of what Lucy had just told her slowly sank into her brain, while panic rose in her throat.

"Dear, you must believe me when I tell you I did not plan for this to happen." Lucy bit her lip and glanced to the side. "Not this soon, at any rate."

Erienne braced a hand against her bedchamber wall, her knees gone weak and watery. When Lucy returned from her talk with her husband, she'd asked Anna to watch the children a bit longer and then motioned for Erienne to follow her out of the nursery.

They'd walked back down the corridor to Erienne's bedchamber, and once they'd reached it, Lucy had opened the door and motioned her inside. Erienne thought the duchess's behavior slightly odd, but it hadn't been until Lucy turned to her with a worried look on her face that Erienne had become truly concerned. She'd seen many expressions on the duchess's face since she'd met her, but worry was never one of them.

"What is it?" Erienne asked, her heart beating faster.

Lucy bit her lip and wrung her hands, two other things Erienne had never seen the duchess do.

"Derek just..." Lucy cleared her throat, "informed me of something important you should know."

"Important? How?" But cold dread had already begun to creep along Erienne's spine. Even before Lucy said the words, Erienne had guessed them.

"It turns out ... Collin is here," Lucy said.

And that was when Erienne slid down the wall to sit in a heap on the floor like a rag doll. No doubt her new employer thought she was daft, but at the moment, her entire body felt as if it was without bones. Her breathing came in short spurts that hurt her chest.

"Collin? Hunt? Is here? Now?" she echoed what she'd already said, something in the back of her brain prompting the words as if they would make more sense or seem more real if she repeated them aloud.

"Yes." Lucy nodded. She lowered herself to sit on the floor across from Erienne and spread her green skirts around her. "It's true. I'm sorry. I can see this is upsetting to you."

"I'm not upset," Erienne blurted. "I'm ..." What in heaven's name was she? She had no idea. Angry? No. Sad? Absolutely not. Upset? That would mean she cared, and she did *not* care. Surprised. Yes. That was it. Merely surprised. She hadn't been expecting to encounter Collin so soon. That was all. Lucy had promised her she needn't worry about it, and—No. No. She wasn't worried, either. That would also imply she cared. And she did *not*.

"Dear, forgive me for pointing it out, but the fact that you're sitting on the floor upon hearing the news belies your statement that you're not upset," Lucy pointed out.

Erienne met her sympathetic stare. "I'm sorry. I am. I'm just … surprised." Yes. *Surprised* was the word she intended to use and keep using. *Surprise* was her emotion and her only emotion.

"I know it must be difficult for you to contemplate seeing him again after so many years," the duchess continued. "But sometimes we encounter people from our past for a reason, and while it may seem uncomfortable at first, perhaps it's precisely what you need. Fate rarely makes mistakes."

Erienne sat in stunned silence for a moment before she said, "With all due respect to both you and fate, Lucy, I'm not certain precisely what I need at the moment, but I'm fairly certain that is not it."

Lucy reached out and squeezed Erienne's hand. "Your skin is cold as snow, dear. Please believe me when I tell you that Collin had written Derek to say he was coming, and Derek failed to mention it to me."

Erienne nodded. She believed the other woman was telling the truth. Truly, she did. But that didn't make the news any less … surprising. "Was that why Derek looked angry when he saw me?"

Lucy winced. "Not exactly. You see … I had failed to tell him I hired you, and we both realized that the potential reunion between you and Collin might be … awkward."

Awkward? That was certainly one way to describe it. "I see. So this means … this means that … Collin doesn't know I'm here?"

"Not yet," Lucy said. "Derek went to find him and tell him."

At that news, Erienne leaned her head back against the wall with a solid thump and closed her eyes.

～

THE AIR HAD BEEN SUCKED from Collin's body. He couldn't breathe, could barely think. He'd heard his brother's words correctly, at least he thought he had, but while they played themselves over and over in his mind, they still did not make much sense.

"Lucy has hired Erienne Stone as the children's governess?" he repeated numbly.

"That's correct." Derek paced in front of the study fireplace, his face lined with regret. "I swear to you, Collin, I had no idea Lucy had done it until I went to find her after you arrived this morning."

Collin's jaw tightened even more. "We *are* speaking of the same Erienne Stone we used to know in Brighton?"

Derek nodded curtly. "Yes."

"You're certain of it?"

Derek clasped his hands behind his back. "I met her myself. It's Miss Stone, from Brighton."

Collin studied his brother through narrowed eyes. "You cannot possibly mean to tell me this is a complete coincidence."

Derek shook his head. "I wouldn't insult your intelligence that way. Lucy was looking at letters from potential governesses last week, and I went through some of them with her. When I saw Miss Stone's name, I mentioned that I knew her."

"You mentioned that *I* knew her, you mean," Collin said in a low voice.

His brother nodded. "Yes. My apologies. I truly never believed Lucy would hire her. I even made her promise she wouldn't choose Miss Stone because of her connection with you."

Collin blew out a deep breath. He was still trying to wrap his mind around this amazing news, and he wasn't at all certain how he felt yet. "Lucy is Lucy, Derek."

Derek hung his head. "I know. I truly am sorry. If I'd had any idea this would have happened—"

"What?" Collin cracked a smile. "You would have put your foot down? I'm not certain Lucy would have listened to you even then."

Derek sighed and shook his head. "It's true. But I love that woman madly no matter what sort of trouble she gets us all into from time to time. Look, I told Lucy we can keep you and Miss Stone separated. It shouldn't be much trouble, and I can—"

"Does Eri …" Collin cleared his throat. "Does Miss Stone know I'm here?"

Derek blew out a breath. "Lucy is telling her now."

CHAPTER NINE

"I insist you come to dinner with us," Lucy said as Erienne raised herself from the floor and made her way to the bed, where she promptly plopped atop the mattress.

She glanced at her new employer, suddenly anxious. "Are you *mad*?" Drat. The question sprang from her mouth before she had a chance to examine it. Lucy might have just informed her that Collin was in the same house, but Erienne had little intention of purposely meeting him. And she had *no* intention of sharing a meal with him, for heaven's sake. She cleared her throat. "What I meant to say was that I regret if this disappoints you, your grace, but no, I will absolutely not come to dinner."

Lucy nodded. "I understand it might be difficult at first, but I think it's best if you see Collin and clear the air. It will make the next fortnight less awkward for both of you."

"There's no reason in the world the next fortnight should be awkward," Erienne said, trying her best to sound nonchalant. "I'll be spending my time with the children, and no doubt he'll be spending time with you and Derek. There's little cause for our paths to cross."

Lucy gave her a look that clearly indicated she thought Erienne was trying too hard with the nonchalance. "Wouldn't you rather get the meeting over with? We can have a nice meal and all catch up. That doesn't have to be awkward, either."

Erienne straightened her shoulders. "I am employed as a governess at this house. Eating meals as a guest is inappropriate."

Lucy blinked at her. "Who says so? You're the childhood friend of my husband and his brother, and your father is a baron, according to Derek. There's no reason in the world I cannot or should not invite you to our dinner table to share a meal with old friends."

"I'd rather not." Her reply was succinct, and hopefully would put an end to Lucy's badgering.

"What if I insist?" Lucy countered.

Erienne pressed her fingertips to her temples where a headache was quickly forming. "I cannot imagine Collin would relish a dinner with the hired help."

"Nonsense." Lucy crossed her arms over her chest and made a little huffing noise. "You're being stubborn and ridiculous. In fact, I'd say you're making far too much of this. If your past with Collin is nothing, as you say it is, why would you object so strongly to a dinner with him?"

Drat. The duchess made sense, too much sense, and she'd just made the one argument Erienne could hardly refute without making it seem as if she cared far more than she was telling herself she did.

"It's only one dinner," Lucy continued. "It doesn't need to be such a bother."

Erienne contemplated the matter for a moment. Perhaps it would be for the best. Have dinner, greet each other, pretend as if nothing had ever happened, and then go about their business for the next fortnight. If she was fortunate, she might not even see Collin again, or only in passing.

She sighed. "Very well, one dinner. If you insist."

A triumphant smile spread across Lucy's face. "Excellent. Now, you must come with me to my rooms. I'll have my maid fix your hair, and I insist upon you wearing one of my gowns."

Erienne arched a brow. "That sounds an awful lot as if I'd be trying too hard."

"You're an old friend, and we're merely going to put some rouge on your cheeks and pin up your hair. If you also borrow some jewelry, so be it."

"Lucy?" Erienne dragged out the word and gave her a skeptical glare. "You wouldn't be trying to make me beautiful, would you?"

"Erienne, darling, you're already beautiful. I'm merely going to make Collin wish he hadn't waited so long to see you again."

And suddenly, Erienne knew she couldn't win. Lucy was a cheerful squall, blowing through the peaceful ocean of her life, and there was no way to stop the waves that would inevitably toss Erienne to and fro. Reluctantly, she stood and trailed the duchess out of the room and toward the other woman's bedchamber. Erienne highly doubted rouge and a pretty gown would make Collin wish anything. She would end up regretting this. She knew she would. It had been an age since she'd dressed in finery and attended an elegant dinner with people of the Quality. Would she even remember how to go about it? And what sort of small talk could she possibly invent over dinner with Collin and Derek Hunt?

One could only imagine the sort of beautification the duchess had in store for her, but Erienne had already learned quite well that Lucy got what Lucy wanted, and apparently, at the moment, Lucy wanted to make Erienne look like a fine lady instead of a governess.

They entered the duchess's rooms, where Lucy proceeded to drag Erienne by the hand into her large dressing room. She threw open the doors of several enormous wardrobes to reveal gowns of every fabric and color hanging inside. The space looked like a dressmaker's shop. Erienne wanted to turn in a circle and look at each and every one of the lovely gowns.

"I do believe you're my size before I had the children." Lucy plunked her hands on her hips and sized up Erienne. "I'd hate for all these pretty gowns to go to waste." She rushed over to pull out a gorgeous, ice-blue satin concoction with silver trim and a silver sarsnet overskirt. "This will go perfectly with your eyes. Oh, and with diamonds, it'll be exquisite!"

Erienne shook her head and bit her lip to hide a smile. She shouldn't be enjoying this, but she couldn't help herself. In her heart, she was still a girl who liked to look pretty once in a while. And the mention of diamonds made her the tiniest bit giddy.

"I have the most lovely matching silver slippers with bows on the ends to go with this," Lucy continued.

"It's not too much, is it?" Erienne asked in a doubtful tone.

"Not at all." Lucy waggled her eyebrows. "You want to see the diamonds, don't you?"

It was official. Erienne was Cinderella and Lucy was her fairy godmother. "Very well," Erienne said, finally warming to the topic. "Show me the diamonds."

Lucy gave a small squeal of excitement. She rang for her maid and asked the woman to gather a necklace and matching earbobs. Then she escorted Erienne over to the dressing table and forced her to sit. "I think a chignon for your hair tonight, don't you? Elegant, but simple." She picked up a brush, plucked the pins out of Erienne's serviceable coiffure, and began brushing the long, blond locks.

"Oh, Lucy," Erienne said with a laugh, closing her eyes and leaning back. "I know I'm going to regret this later, but it is fun, isn't it?"

"One never regrets a beautification, dear. And the fun hasn't even started yet."

Erienne opened her eyes and stared at her reflection in the mirror. She finally allowed a large smile to spread across her face. She was thinner than she used to be. She was older than she used to be. Would Collin still find her attractive? Would she still find him attractive?

"So," Lucy said, after the maid returned with the jewels. She held up the gorgeous necklace, and Erienne's eyes widened in amazement. "What exactly happened between you and Collin all those years ago?"

CHAPTER TEN

Brighton, June 1807

Erienne tossed her schoolbooks aside and flew up the stairs to her bedchamber. She had just turned sixteen, and was bored stiff learning comportment and French when she'd much rather be outside in the fresh air, breathing in the scent of the sea, the wind whipping her hair. But today, today was a much better day than the long boring days before it, because Collin was back in town. He'd been gone to the army for nearly three years and was on leave for a fortnight. He'd written to her as he'd promised, letters that weren't personal in nature because he knew her parents would read them.

Her parents were none too pleased with her infatuation with one of the Hunt brothers. The boys came from the family of a disgraced army officer who drank too much and treated his sons poorly, but that hadn't stopped Erienne from falling madly in love with Collin. Of course they were only friends at first, but she couldn't recall a time when she hadn't admired him. Sometime around her thirteenth birthday, when Collin was sixteen, just before he'd left for the army, they'd begun a game. One of them would write something on a small slip of paper, a challenge. Whatever the words, the other must comply or forfeit.

Collin had slipped her a note when he'd seen her in church that Sunday. It contained only six words: *Meet me by the sycamore tree*. She hadn't had to ask which sycamore tree. A huge one graced the area behind the church in the little grove just past the cemetery. She'd feigned the need to use the necessary and hurried outside to the tree.

It was there, as they wiped tears away from their eyes and said their goodbyes, that Erienne had lifted up on her tiptoes and whispered in Collin's ear that she would love him forever.

Their first kiss should have been on her sixteenth birthday, but Collin was off training at the time. She'd written him in the code they'd developed. Every tenth word of their letters spelled out a sentence with their true feelings, and Collin had promised her secretly, by writing back in the same code, that he would kiss her for her sixteenth birthday present, even if belatedly.

Erienne had been working on her excuse to her mother and governess this particular morning. She'd begun bringing food and some old clothing to the poorhouse on Wednesday afternoons, after her studies ended, and she intended to do the same thing today. Only she planned to cut short her visit with Mrs. Elmsly and the other ladies at the poorhouse to meet Collin at their appointed spot.

Erienne's middle was a mass of nerves as she brushed her hair fifty times, wrapped it into a chignon, and pinned it atop her head. She smoothed her hands down her white gown and pinched her cheeks to give them color. Then she hurried down to the kitchens to gather the basket Cook prepared each week for the poorhouse.

"Mother," she called as she climbed the stairs to the main level of the house, "I'm off to see Mrs. Elmsly."

A general affirmative sound came from the direction of the front salon, where her mother wrote her correspondence on Wednesday afternoons.

Erienne was out the front door and halfway down the street in minutes, a thrill of freedom coursing through her veins.

A short time later, she arrived at the poorhouse, not far from the church. She handed her basket to a grateful Mrs. Elmsly and asked how all of the children were doing, but she could barely contain her excitement, and it wasn't long before she said, "Good day, Mrs. Elmsly. I must get back."

She didn't allow the woman to protest. Instead, Erienne hiked her shawl around her shoulders and hurried out the door. She made her way down the street as she always did, but when she came to the corner where the little white-washed church sat, she went left toward the church instead of right toward her father's house.

She glanced around to make certain no one had seen her. There were a few people out running errands, and Mr. Sanderson was herding a small group of sheep across the road in the opposite direction, but otherwise, no one seemed to care where she was going. She hurried along the side of the church and continued past the copse of trees behind the small cemetery until she spotted the tall branches of the sycamore tree. *Their* sycamore tree ... hers and Collin's.

He was standing there, waiting for her in his uniform, looking so tall and handsome and formal in his red jacket, white breeches, and black boots, polished to a shine. Her heart swelled.

A twig snapped under her slipper and he turned toward her. He held a bouquet of wildflowers in his hands. She loved flowers. Especially wild flowers. White, purple, and green.

They were lovely. As soon as he realized it was her, a wide smile spread across his face. A smile that took her breath away. Collin had always been good-looking, but now he was even more so. Standing a few inches over six feet, he had brown hair, a perfectly straight nose, and dark slashes for brows that rested above jade-green eyes that missed nothing.

"Erienne," he breathed.

She ran into his arms, and he picked her up and spun her around.

"I've missed you so, Collin."

"I've missed you, too." He set her gingerly back on her feet and cupped her elbows, looking down into her face. "You look beautiful, as always."

"So do you," she replied with a laugh.

"You received my last letter?"

"Yes." She nodded. "I'm certain Mother doesn't know the code. She even remarked on how similar our letters sound. I think she meant boring."

"Similar and dull," Collin said, laughing. "Precisely how we intend to write them." He paused, and the look on his face turned serious. "I'm sorry I missed your birthday."

Erienne's heart skipped a beat. This was it. He was going to kiss her. "You can make it up to me."

"How?"

She pressed a tiny bit of parchment into his hand, burying her nose in her shawl to hide the blush burning her cheeks.

Kiss me, the note read.

He lifted his gaze to look at her with love shining in his eyes, then he lowered his head toward hers, and Erienne lifted her arms to wrap around his neck. The moment his lips brushed hers, a jolt of heat rocked through her and settled between her legs.

As though he sensed her inner reaction, he pulled her

tight against his hard body, and Erienne moaned. Her arms tightened around his neck and she clung to him while his tongue slid between her lips to explore her mouth. She hadn't thought a kiss could be so invasive—or that she'd enjoy the invasion so much. Then his mouth slanted across hers and the kiss turned into something else entirely. Pure waves of lust streaked through her body as Collin kissed her again and again. One of his rough hands tenderly cupped her cheek, while the other held her snugly against him, somehow aligning every inch of their bodies though he was so tall and she so small. And she followed every movement he made, every restless shift, as if they were dancing.

When he sank to his knees in the cool grass, he took her with him, so tightly entangled were their bodies. And when the world tilted and she felt the soft, fragrant ground beneath her, she didn't think, couldn't think, because Collin was atop her, his weight welcome and warm. They kissed again and again, starved for each other after so many years of wanting —and then the laughter came, born of pure happiness. They rolled in the grass, laughing and clutching each other, lust melding into joy, until finally Collin lifted off her and flopped onto his side to stare at her.

"I wish I didn't have to leave you again." He was panting as he pulled a twig out of her coiffure and tossed it away.

"I wish you never had to leave again." Erienne traced the line of his brow with one trembling finger, her bliss fading with the thought of being parted from him.

Collin pulled her against his chest and rested his chin atop her head. They lay like that, wrapped in each other's arms, for as long as they dared. Dusk had begun to fall by the time Erienne murmured, "I'd better get back."

She saw him three more times during those two weeks. Theirs were always stolen moments they had to eke out around duty and family, but looking back, she recognized their last encounter was a sign of things to come.

"Mother says my debut is the most important thing I'll ever do, and I cannot let up on my studies lest I fail to find a decent husband. Can you imagine?" Erienne didn't know why she'd brought up her debut. It was at least two years off. She supposed she wanted to see how Collin would react to the notion that she was to be put on the marriage mart.

His dark brows lowered. "Whom do your parents wish you to marry?"

She'd been so nonchalant that day, waving her hand in the air. Words had tripped off her tongue so easily, as if they had no meaning. "Someone of the *Quality*, of course." She'd sneered the word 'Quality.' None of that had ever mattered to her. She'd known she would marry Collin since she'd been a girl. She didn't give a whit what her parents thought was best for her.

"Of course," Collin said, but a brief flash of hurt highlighted his fine features.

"Collin?" They were lounging in the grass by the tree again. She turned toward him. "You know I don't care about any of that, don't you? My debut and all the rest of it."

"You should care, Erienne," he replied solemnly.

"But I don't. I never have. I love you." She'd wrapped her arms around his neck and pressed her lips to his. He'd returned the kiss, passionately. They were going to be together forever.

"You love me too, don't you?" she asked after the kiss ended, just needing to be reassured, to hear it again.

"Of course I do, Air."

"And we're going to marry one day, you and I."

His only response had been to pull her closer into his arms and squeeze her tight.

~

THEY CONTINUED their code-filled correspondence over the next two years. Erienne resumed her lessons with her governess, and as her eighteenth birthday approached, she wrote Collin about the preparations for her going to court to make her debut. Mother, of course, had approved of those letters because she saw it as Erienne letting poor Collin Hunt know that she intended to marry someone of the Quality, as she should. But in the code within the letters, she'd continued to write things such as, *I love you, Collin. I miss you, Collin. I cannot wait to see you again.*

Collin had written back with news of his training and deployments and even his first promotion, one that failed to impress Erienne's parents. "He's still a Hunt," Mother had said, turning up her nose as if she smelled something disagreeable.

As her debut approached, Erienne noticed that Collin's letters arrived less often. She told herself he was preoccupied with his assignments, and she herself was terribly busy doing a hundred silly, unimportant things, like picking out the trim for her ball gown and choosing feathers for her hair for the debut at the palace. She wrote of these things to Collin, while his letters dried up.

Finally, the summer after her eighteenth birthday, after she'd made her debut and spent the Season fending off offers from a lot of useless gentlemen who'd never known a hard day's work, Collin wrote to tell her he was coming home again.

Elation unlike anything she'd ever felt had exploded in her chest. Now that she was of age, they could marry. It would take some convincing of her parents, of course, but Erienne was confident that together, she and Collin would make them see how deeply they loved each other, and how intent they were upon spending their lives together.

The first night after Collin's return, Erienne found the little scrap of paper tucked into a knot outside her bedchamber window. *Meet me at the sycamore tree*. That afternoon after church, she gathered her skirts and ran there.

Collin was there, as always, but now twenty-one years old, and looking as handsome as ever. Her heart skipped a beat. This was it. Their future could begin. They would never be separated again. She ran into his arms and he spun her around like he had two years ago, only this time when he let her down into the grass, he immediately kissed her until her head spun, too.

"It's time," she said breathlessly. "Time to tell my parents we intend to marry."

He gathered her anew in his arms and kissed her once more. She hadn't known it at the time, but it was to be their last kiss. God, if only she'd known. If only she'd been older, wiser, she would have handled the entire thing differently.

"I love you, Erienne," he'd breathed. "I'll always love you."

"I love you too, Collin." Her brow furrowed as she stared at him. The way he'd spoken sounded strange, off.

He hung his head. "But we cannot marry."

"What?" The word came out of her throat in a whisper. She was certain she hadn't heard him correctly. She couldn't possibly have.

"We cannot marry, Erienne."

She searched his face. Surely he was only teasing her. "What? Why not?"

"It wouldn't be fair to you."

"Collin ..." She clasped a hand to her breast, struggling for air as if she were drowning. "What are you saying? You love me, don't you?"

"I'll love you forever, Air." He traced the line of her cheek with one finger in that old, familiar way of his.

She swallowed hard. "Then why are you saying this? Why can't we be together?"

"My life ... in the army. It's difficult, and I won't be home much. I'm soon to be shipped off to the Continent. I will be in danger."

She shook her head impatiently. "I know all of this, Collin. You've told me. I don't care."

"But you will care, Air. You will care eventually. You deserve someone who will love you and be with you, treat you like a princess. You deserve one of those suitors who has money and ... a title." His throat worked.

Tears stung her eyes like needles. She fought against them, clenching her jaw. "You know I don't care about titles."

"You deserve the best," he said low, turning away to push his hands through his hair in a gesture of firm but melancholy resolution. "That's not me."

Tears flowed freely down her face. It *was* him. It was. Why did he refuse to believe that? She shook her head. "Don't do this."

"I should go." His voice was flat, hard. He turned back to her abruptly, grabbed her hand, and pressed a small slip of paper into it. And then, just like that, he was gone.

She hung her head, hot tears squeezing through her lashes, and waited until she could no longer hear his bootsteps crunching through the twigs. Only then did she open her palm and flip over the tiny slip of paper.

Three words. Each one ripped through her heart anew.

Let me go.

CHAPTER ELEVEN

Collin couldn't recall the last time he'd been nervous. Bloody hell, a seasoned spy didn't succumb to nerves. Ever. But as he sat next to Derek in his brother's dining room, waiting for Lucy and Erienne to join them for dinner, he felt as unsettled as he had when he was a young man, the day he'd first kissed Erienne by the sycamore tree.

Erienne. He couldn't believe he was about to see her again after all these years. The day he'd told her he couldn't marry her had been the most excruciating of his entire life. But he'd known then—just as he knew now—it was the right thing to do. The best thing. Perhaps not for him, but certainly for her. He loved her enough to let her go. He always had.

In the months leading up to her debut, she'd written to him all about the fancy gowns her mother had bought her for her debutante ball to be held in London. Clearly, Erienne was meant for that life. Her father was a baron, and she was gorgeous and perfect. She shouldn't waste herself on the likes of him, the boy from the bad family in town. It had been selfish of him to love her. He had to let her go.

He'd begun writing her less often, trying to wean himself from the joy of her regular correspondence, although he knew it would nearly kill him to stop receiving her letters. Those letters had been the only things to get him through some very dark days. He'd worked his arse off, doing his best to rise through the ranks as quickly as possible to be worthy of Erienne, to be someone her parents could accept, someone she could be proud of. But that summer, after her debut, he'd received a letter from Erienne's father, dashing all of his hopes.

Baron Stone had begun the letter cordially enough. He asked after Collin's health and indicated he'd heard Collin was doing quite well for himself in the army. But quickly, the baron made the purpose of the letter quite clear.

It seems Erienne has a schoolgirl infatuation with you. I think we would both agree that she should be with someone of her status. Quite simply, she has received multiple offers of marriage and refused them all because of you, Lieutenant Hunt. This is to her detriment. Her mother and I ask that you desist in your correspondence with her in order to allow her the space she needs to find a suitable husband.

THE WORD *suitable* had sliced like a dagger through Collin's heart. Of course he wasn't suitable, and no matter how high he rose in the army, he never would be. To the Stones, he would always be the Hunt boy from the tiny, ramshackle cottage on the far side of town.

He'd written back, agreeing with Baron Stone that Erienne deserved the best husband in the world. He'd told the baron he would tell Erienne in person during his next leave, which was coming up. He refused to tell her in a letter like a coward. Baron Stone had agreed to that stipulation.

The afternoon Collin had written *Let me go* on that slip of paper and pressed it into Erienne's hand was the worst day of his life.

He'd left the next morning, gone back to the army early because he couldn't stand to be so near her and not see her. Worse, he didn't trust himself in the same town with her. He might forget himself and go find her and tell her he'd been insane and hadn't meant a word of it. He took a swallow of his drink. It burned a path through his insides as he stared out the dining room window at the night. He saw nothing in that dark glass but his own reflection, and for the first time, he recognized a hardness to his features he knew wasn't put there by war with his fellow man, but by war with his own traitorous heart.

Erienne had been the only wonderful thing in his childhood. She'd been the promise he'd kept in his heart all these years, and he'd been forced to let her go. It was for her sake, however. That was the only thing that comforted him. He'd always believed that someday she would thank him for giving her the chance to live the life she truly deserved.

His mouth twisted in a humorless smile. He'd had a moment of insanity, however. After that day, he hadn't received another letter from her, but he'd come home that Christmastide and rushed to her house, wanting to tell her he'd been a fool, wanting to ask her if she would forgive him and marry him after all.

He'd been shown into the Stones' drawing room by their house steward and waited with his hat in his hands, his palms sweaty, before Lady Stone came marching into the room, her face tight. "Lieutenant Hunt," she intoned, not sounding particularly pleased to see him. "To what do I owe the pleasure?"

"I've come to see Erienne," Collin replied.

"Erienne?" A brief look of surprise flashed across the woman's face.

"Yes. Is she here?"

Lady Stone composed her features into a mask. "She is not."

"May I wait?"

The lady lifted her chin. "I'm afraid you'd be waiting quite some time, Mr. Hunt. Erienne no longer lives here. She's moved to Shropsbury."

"Shropsbury?" A mixture of surprise and concern clutched at his throat.

"Yes." The woman's gaze dropped to the floor. "To live with her *husband*."

The statement gutted him. Collin nearly doubled over in pain. "She's married?" he asked to clarify the news to his own stumbling brain.

"Yes." Lady Stone folded her hands together. She still didn't meet his eyes.

"Who? Who did she marry?" He couldn't stop himself from asking the awful question.

"Ah ... Viscount Tinworth. Do you know him?"

The name was completely unfamiliar to Collin. But he'd hardly taken stock of London's finest. "No."

"They're quite happy together. I expect news of a baby any day now," Lady Stone added.

Collin's jaw turned to marble. "I see." He turned on his heel and headed toward the door. "Thank you, Lady Stone. I'll show myself out."

He walked all the way home without a coat, kicking his boots through the newly fallen snow. It had been madness for him to try to come back after all these months. Erienne had married someone of her class. She was out of his reach. As it should be, for the best.

That had been the last time he'd ever attempted to contact Erienne Stone.

And now they were about to meet again, a hapless reconciliation hardly of their own making. For some insane reason, he'd decided to wear his uniform to dinner tonight. As if the medals on his jacket could protect him from ... what? The decisions of his past? He clutched his drink. God, but his nerves felt as if they could wind up his insides and strangle a cry of utter frustration from his throat. He took another long draught to stifle it, to set those nerves afire and destroy the emotions. He emptied his glass.

And he waited.

CHAPTER TWELVE

At last, the moment came.

Such moments are always less than one expects, Collin thought later, and somehow so much more.

At the flash of movement in the dining room doorway, Collin immediately pushed back his chair and stood to greet the duchess and, finally, Erienne.

She wore an ice-blue gown, one worthy of a fine lady. The kind of gown he'd always pictured her in when he thought of her married in Shropsbury.

Apparently she was a governess now, however. He'd half-expected her to be wearing a serviceable gown with an apron like the ones he'd seen Miss Langley sport a time or two. But Erienne stood there looking heartbreakingly beautiful in that gown, and for a moment he thought this meeting, the one where he stood in his dress uniform and she in ice-blue perfection, was as it should have been all along if he'd been able to attend her debut, to court her as he'd always desired.

She was thinner than she used to be. But the same knowing, lovely blue gaze shined from her delicate features. There were slight, dark smudges under her eyes as if she were tired. Diamonds clung to the fragile bones of her neckline and matching diamonds hung from her ears. Her golden hair was up in a chignon and her lips, pink and full, rested in a straight line, neither smiling nor frowning.

But he recognized the apprehension gathered in the lines of her familiar face.

She glanced at him and then away, so quickly he'd barely seen it. He wouldn't have noticed at all if he hadn't been watching her so closely.

"Collin." Lucy came to his side of the table and gave him a hug. "It's lovely to see you again. It's been far too long." She turned to Erienne. "You remember Miss Stone, I believe."

He cleared his throat, not trusting his voice, but having no choice. "Of course."

"Erienne." Lucy turned back to face her. "You recall General Hunt?"

"General?" Erienne's startled eyes flickered to meet Collin's, and the words seem to die on her lips before she found them again. "I'd no idea."

"Yes," Derek said as he held out Lucy's chair, leaving Collin to hurry around the table and pull out Erienne's seat. "Collin is quite a high-ranking official at the Home Office now. Of course the position has come at the expense of his social life."

They all took their seats. Derek at the head of the table, Lucy at the foot, with Collin to Derek's left and Erienne to Derek's right, directly across from Collin. The footmen rushed to place napkins on their laps and fill their wine-glasses for the first course.

Erienne kept her eyes trained on her plate, though her chin took on a subtle, stubborn set that Collin instantly recognized. "Yes," she said primly, "I do seem to recall Mr.

Hunt placing emphasis on his position in the army over his own personal interests."

And off went the warm light of sentimentality he'd foolishly been entertaining. Collin grabbed the half-poured wine glass in front of him and nearly downed its entire contents.

Lucy's bright eyes glanced back and forth between Collin and Erienne. "Yes, well, Collin's been forced on holiday. That's why he's here at the moment, isn't that right, Coll?"

"Indeed." He couldn't stop glancing at Erienne. Despite her apparent state of pique, she was even more beautiful than she'd been when they were young. More so, even, with the tiny lines near her eyes and the sides of her mouth, borne of too many smiles—and perhaps too many frowns. She looked as if she'd seen pain. He hoped he hadn't been the cause of it.

"A general and high-ranking officer in the Home Office," Erienne echoed as the footmen set a bowl of turtle soup in front of each of them. "How ever did you manage that, Mr. Hunt?"

"Years and years of hard work, Miss Stone."

"And what about your *wife*?" Erienne's polite but pointed query held the edge of a knife. "Is she resigned to the amount of time you spend away from home?"

"I've never married," Collin replied, meeting her gaze. Was it his imagination or did relief glint in her eyes?

"Collin was a spy in the wars," Derek added in an obvious attempt to change the subject.

The briefest flash of concern passed over Erienne's face before she seemed to school her features. "I did not know that. In fact, I haven't heard any details of Mr. Hunt's life since we last saw each other in Brighton. What's it been? Fourteen years now?" She took a deep sip from her wine glass.

Fourteen years, one month, and sixteen days, Collin thought, but who was counting? "Something like that." He lifted his spoon. "Speaking of work," he continued, "I was surprised to hear that you've been employed as a governess, Miss Stone."

"Yes, I left for Baron Hilltop's house the summer after I turned eighteen," she replied sweetly, as if they both didn't know precisely what that summer had meant to them. "I've been there since."

Collin frowned, his soup spoon paused halfway to his lips. "What about the viscount?"

"The viscount?" Erienne's brows lowered. "I never worked for a viscount, only Baron Hilltop."

Collin ate his soup in silence for a few moments, allowing that news to settle in. She'd been in Shropsbury working as a governess all this time? Never married to a viscount? Why, that would mean ...

Her mother lied. Of course her awful mother had lied! And he, the young fool that he'd been, had believed her. But why had Erienne not married? Why had she taken a position as a governess instead of accepting one of the offers from the many gentlemen who'd courted her that year?

Collin stared unseeing into his soup bowl and swallowed the hard lump that had formed in his throat. He had a terrible feeling he knew precisely why.

CHAPTER THIRTEEN

Erienne could barely breathe. Being this close to Collin again, even after all these years, was too much. She wasn't over it. She wasn't over him. She never had been. And what in heaven's name had he meant, asking her about a viscount?

Lucy might think this little dinner party was a good idea, but Erienne now realized it was anything but. She had to get away. She glanced over at Collin again. She'd been trying to eye him surreptitiously when she thought he wasn't looking, but he kept catching her. It hurt to look at him, but she couldn't stop herself. The years had been nothing but kind to him. He was even more handsome than he'd been in his youth, his cheekbones more pronounced, his green eyes even more thoughtful and wise, and he had an air of confidence and authority about him that hadn't been there when they were younger.

The man was a general now, and a high-ranking official in the Home Office. She wasn't surprised, not truly. Just as she hadn't been surprised to learn Derek had become a war-hero duke. But Collin wasn't in the papers the way his brother had been. His exploits hadn't been famous for good reason. He'd been a spy.

She shuddered to think about how much danger he'd probably been in over the years. No doubt he'd been in mortal peril a time or two. He'd been promoted to the rank of general, and from the look of the large number of medals on his red woolen jacket, he was quite someone. She didn't know a great deal about the Home Office, but being an official there had to mean he was both valued and powerful.

"What are your plans while you're here, Collin?" Lucy asked, clearly attempting to keep the conversation afloat.

"My orders are to relax," Collin replied with the ghost of a laugh. "I'm not certain that is possible."

"You should go fishing." Lucy signaled one of the footmen to refill Collin's wine glass. "The creek is full of fish this time of year."

Collin inclined his head. "I might." He glanced at Erienne. "I would also like very much to see the children."

Erienne froze. Of course he would want to see the children. She tried not picture him filling the nursery space with his wide shoulders and appealing presence.

"Go up and see them in the morning, first thing," Lucy said cheerfully. "They'll be thrilled. We haven't yet told them you've come. We wanted it to be a surprise."

"I'll do that," Collin replied. "If that's all right with you, Miss Stone."

Erienne forced a smile to her lips. "Of course," she murmured, but she couldn't play this particular game any longer. She had to get away from this table. This dinner. She couldn't pretend they were all simply old friends, catching up.

She stood and tossed her napkin to her chair. "If you'll excuse me, I'll just go check on the children now. Thank you for a lovely dinner, your grace."

71

She hurried from the room before any of them could make noises to the contrary. In her wake, she heard the screech of chair legs as the men stood, and no doubt that utterance of dismay was Lucy, whose matchmaking plans had been laid to waste.

Erienne breathed a sigh of relief when she reached the corridor. Her excuse had been a thinly veiled reason to flee, and the rest of the table knew it, too, but she didn't care. She couldn't sit across the table from Collin one more moment and listen to stories about how successful he'd become in a career that he'd chosen over her.

She hurried up the stairs to the children's nursery. Anna was there, putting away some of the toys the children had used earlier. "They're in bed, Miss," she said to Erienne's questioning look.

"Thank you, Anna, for watching them while I was at dinner." She hung her head and left the room. The children didn't even need her. What should she do with herself? She wandered back to her own room and opened the door. The bed had been turned down and candles were lit on either side of its curtained expanse. A soft glow came from both the sitting room and the dressing room.

She made her way to the dressing room and glanced around the space. Her trunk had been unpacked earlier by a maid named Millie, who Lucy had introduced as the one Erienne should ask for anything she needed. Her serviceable gowns, far different from the one she wore at the moment, hung in the wardrobe. Her three little reticules had been lined up on a shelf beneath the gowns.

She bent and picked up the little bag she used the least, pulled the string apart to loosen it, and fished her fingers inside until she located the tiny piece of paper with the smudged ink. She pulled it out and stared at it, a humorless smile touching her lips as she rubbed her finger across the too-familiar words.

Let me go.

The words Collin had written to her fourteen years ago. She'd kept the note all this time. She only looked at it at moments like these, when memories of him overwhelmed her. She'd been able to let the man go, but she'd kept the scrap of paper. How was that for irony?

Tears sprang to Erienne's eyes, but she quickly blinked them away. She refused to cry—hadn't cried since that summer, fourteen years ago. She'd arranged to take the position at the Hilltops' without her mother knowing and had left her parents a note. Her mother had written her soon after, begging her to come back and choose from her suitors. Erienne needed to marry someone wealthy, her mother claimed, because her father's business dealings had soured of late and while their name was reputable, their fortune was quickly dwindling. But Erienne couldn't do it. She couldn't pledge herself to a man she didn't love, even after the one she did love had asked her to let him go.

Years later, when her brother had returned from war grievously injured, she promised to send home as much of her wages as she could spare to help care for Peter. It was her choice to remain a spinster that had caused her family further financial hardship, and she couldn't bear to allow her beloved sibling to suffer as a result.

Erienne pushed the small slip of paper back inside the reticule and returned it to the shelf. Then she wandered back into her bedchamber and stared blindly at the bed for a few moments. She knew sleep would be a stranger tonight, but she refused to return to the dining room. Instead, she trailed her way down the corridor to the servants' staircase at the back of the house, descended to the main floor, and slipped outside.

Slowly making her way around the side of the building to the manicured gardens outside the library, she breathed in the jasmine that filled the late-summer night air, and paused to revel in it as she passed beneath a trellis covered in the pungent vine. Moonlight glinted off the dark green leaves.

"There's a sycamore tree by the lake." Collin's deep voice sounded from behind her in the darkness. "I'd invite you there, but something tells me you'd refuse."

Erienne closed her eyes. Pain clenched her heart. He remembered the sycamore tree. "You'd be right," she said without turning.

Gravel crunched beneath his boots as he came closer. "I hope you didn't leave dinner on my account."

What could she possibly say to that? She finally faced him and found him partially lost in shadow. "I ... needed some air."

"Do you want me to leave?" he asked even as he drew nearer.

The question took her by surprise, but she shook her head curtly. "This is your brother's house. I'd never be so rude as to ask you to leave."

"I'd leave if you asked me to, Air." His voice was soft, caring. Heartbreakingly familiar.

She couldn't take it if he called her Air. She concentrated on breathing normally, in and out. "At dinner you asked about a viscount. What did you mean?"

"It doesn't matter now. I realized that I'd been ... misinformed about your whereabouts."

"Misinformed? By whom?"

His gaze captured hers, his eyes glinting in the darkness. "Does it matter after all these years, Erienne?"

She glanced away and kicked at a pebble on the path with her slipper. It did something to her middle to hear her name on his lips. "I suppose it doesn't."

He was close enough now that she could smell his cologne beneath the jasmine, the familiar scent of him she remembered from all those years ago. It catapulted her back in time. She clenched her jaw against the memories that threatened to overwhelm her, fighting to keep from turning to flee.

"I missed you." The warm timber of his voice sent shock waves pounding through her body.

She wrapped her arms around her middle and swallowed hard. "Why would you say that to me, after all these years?" She could hear the anguish in her own voice, but there was nothing to be done. She'd never been anything but truthful with him.

He took a final step toward her, and the heat from his body warmed her cool skin. "Because it's true," he said softly. "Did you miss me?"

She didn't want to answer him. It was unfair of him to ask. But to deny it would be a lie.

He swayed closer, his shadow enveloping her. He lowered his head and lifted her chin with his finger. Every brick in the wall that had surrounded her heart for so long seemed to fly away like so much dust in a brisk wind.

He searched her face in the darkness. "I hurt you, didn't I, Erienne?"

She refused to answer that too. She wouldn't give him the satisfaction of knowing it for certain. "You asked me to let you go, and I did." It was all she would give him, all she would admit.

"I'm sorry," he breathed. "For hurting you, and I'll probably be sorry for this." He closed the few scarce inches between them and kissed her. His lips slanted fiercely over hers, and she clutched at the lapels of his coat to steady herself. They kissed like that, endlessly, before Collin pulled away from her, breathing heavily. He pressed his forehead to hers. "Come with me," he said, tugging her by the hand behind him as he made his way toward the French doors that opened into the house. "I know somewhere even better than the sycamore tree."

Erienne allowed herself to be led, unable—or perhaps merely unwilling—to say a word. They were going somewhere to continue kissing, and possibly to do more. She knew she shouldn't want to, shouldn't accompany him, and yet she couldn't make her mouth speak a protest or her feet stop moving forward. It was if her mind had relinquished its role in making her decisions. Clearly, her body and heart had taken over.

Collin pulled her into a room that a brief glance showed was a library and closed the door behind them. It was completely dark inside, save for the banked fire in the fireplace at the far end. The fire gave a soft glow to the large space, but did not illuminate it. He led her over to a wide leather sofa in the center of the room and drew her back into his arms to kiss her again before urging her down to the cushions. She found herself atop him. His body was hard and hot and he smelled so good. She couldn't get enough of him. He sat up and wrestled out of his coat, never allowing their lips to part, and then he tugged her over him again, this time while he sat at an angle in the turn of the sofa so that she was half atop his lap. It was a most unseemly position ... and she loved every moment of it.

His lips moved to her ear and he sucked in the lobe. "God, Erienne, I missed you. I've wanted you all these years," he whispered.

Oh, God. If only he wouldn't speak, it would be easier to pretend that way. She pressed her mouth against his once more to silence him, so he spoke in a different way—a lover's way. Without hesitation, his strong, rough hand moved to the hem of her skirt and lifted it. He maneuvered them so that they lay side-by-side on the sofa, and his hand made its way up to the juncture between her thighs. She should move away, ask him to stop, but she couldn't force herself to. She wanted his touch, had longed for it for the last fourteen years. Erienne knew the basics of conjugal relations, but not the particulars—these lovely particulars she hadn't imagined could be so thrilling.

"May I touch you, Erienne?"

"Yes." She breathed the word and his fingers deftly pushed aside her shift and drawers. Cool air brushed across the damp, heated flesh between her thighs, and then his touch, and she jolted at that too-intimate, too-wonderful caress, at the circular dance of—was that his thumb? It played her like an instrument, inciting the most restless pleasure with each stroke, over and over.

Erienne wanted to cry out, to beg him to stop, and never to stop. Her head fell back against the side of the sofa and she clenched her eyes shut. Her thighs tensed and she sobbed in the back of her throat. Never in her life had she experienced pleasure like this, and the fact that it was Collin Hunt giving it to her made it all the more bittersweet. Then, somehow, his touch was *within* her too. One long finger perhaps, sliding inside her so easily, so sinuously, she bit her lip to stop her cry. How could this mad pleasure increase? It felt so wonderful.

His hand moved as if to withdraw, and she immediately clamped her thighs around it until it obediently regained its delicious, probing depth within her. She thought he might have released a huff of laughter against her cheek, but then he was whispering hot words in her ear, telling her how beautiful and soft and lovely she was, and she wanted to melt. No moment could have been more perfect, no delight more astonishing ... until his thumb found that *other* spot she'd forgotten about, and circled it, and stroked it, while inside her ... inside her, was it one finger or two that played the perfect notes and drove the music through her body until it was no longer her own? It was too much. The last thing she remembered was the tender press of his kiss on her bowed throat as she thrashed into a blind, mindless pleasure she never had dreamed existed.

A few minutes passed, during which Erienne got her breathing right once more, before she sensed the gentle withdrawal of his touch. Instantly, the insanity of what she'd just allowed whipped through her mind. What in heaven's name had she just done?

She scrambled up from the sofa, righting her skirts and finding herself newly breathless, this time with humiliation. She turned to glare at Collin, though she wasn't entirely certain he could see her face in the dim glow from the fireplace.

She wasn't angry with him. She was angry with herself. How in the space of a few short hours had she allowed Collin Hunt to crawl back into her heart and touch her like that, so ... so wantonly and ... and deliciously? She wanted to sob with self-hatred. She wanted to scream.

Collin slowly rose to his feet and stepped close as if to touch her again. "Erienne, I—"

The crack of her palm striking his cheek was like a shot from a pistol.

He didn't so much as flinch, as though he'd known it was coming, the explosion of rage she could no longer contain. "I'm sorry," he murmured. "I shouldn't have—"

"That wasn't for tonight," she retorted through clenched teeth. "That was for fourteen years ago."

CHAPTER FOURTEEN

Erienne was sitting in the nursery with the children the next morning when Lucy came floating in. She hugged and kissed Mary and Ralph before turning to Erienne. "I do hope you're not angry with me, dear, for suggesting last night's dinner."

"I'm not." How could she be angry with Lucy? The least of the issues with last night had been Lucy insisting Erienne come to dinner.

"I'm so pleased to hear it," the duchess continued. "Derek and Collin were up with the sun and went for a ride, but Collin intends to visit the children before noon."

"Uncle Cawwin is here?" Mary asked, her dark eyebrows rising.

"Yes, darling, your Uncle Collin is here. You'll get to see him soon."

Smiling, Mary clapped her hands together.

"He's only seen Ralph at the christening in London," Lucy said, leaning over and picking up her son. "No doubt he'll be shocked to see how big you've grown, Ralphie." She hoisted the child onto her hip.

The toddler stuck his finger in his mouth and gnawed on it.

Lucy turned back to Erienne. "All that to say, you're welcome to begin your lessons with the children this morning, and then perhaps take them outside for a bit before their visit with Collin. I hate to see them cooped up in the nursery all day, especially when it's so lovely outside."

Erienne nodded. "Perhaps we'll go play by the stream."

"That sounds like an excellent idea. Be certain to take Anna with you," Lucy replied.

After Lucy left, Erienne spent the next two hours going over very basic French words with the children. They stopped for play breaks and to eat a snack sent up by Cook. At ten o'clock, Erienne decided Mary and Ralph had enough for children their ages.

"Pick a toy," she announced. "We'll go to the stream."

Mary clapped her hands. "I'll bwing my dollie." She ran across the room to collect a rag doll that sat on a shelf, its hair a mess of yellow yarn.

Erienne chose some wooden blocks for Ralph and placed them in a basket along with a blanket. She called for Anna, and with the nursemaid leading, their little group left for the stream. They made their way around the side of the house and across the meadow toward a copse of trees that stood near the stream.

When they arrived at the creek, Erienne and Anna spread the large blanket atop the soft grass along the bank and placed the basket on one corner to moor it. The children plopped on the center of the soft quilt and happily played with their toys before Lady Mary asked if she might go to the creek's edge to throw a stone. Apparently, her father had taught her how to do so the last time she'd been there.

"I'll go with you, Mary," Erienne said. She stood and took the little girl's hand.

Mary carried her doll firmly under her other arm as they marched toward the edge of the water. Once they arrived, the child cast about for the perfect stone. Erienne leaned down to find a nice, flat smooth one to show Lady Mary how to skip. Erienne turned away for only a moment when a splash stole her breath. Horrified, Erienne quickly swiveled on her heel. Relief flooded her. Thank heavens, Lady Mary hadn't fallen in. It was her doll.

The little girl pointed into the creek, tears of distress already shining on her cheeks.

Erienne spotted the doll being swiftly carried downstream, and didn't stop to think. She shucked off her slippers and jumped into the ice-cold water. It was a shock to her body, but all she could think about was fetching the little girl's doll.

She was a strong swimmer, but the current was stronger than she'd guessed. She stroked her way toward the doll. Fortunately, its gown had snagged on a tree limb that had fallen across the creek, or she never would have caught up to it.

"I've got it," she called, springing from the water and waving the doll toward Lady Mary and the others, who waited on the far bank many yards away.

Erienne plunged under the water again to swim back, but her own skirt caught on the branch. She dove deeper to locate the snag and free herself, but the water was murky and she couldn't see much. She tried to yank the fabric from the branches, but quickly learned there were many sharp, spiny branches beneath the surface that hadn't been visible from the shore. Freeing herself wouldn't be as simple as she'd hoped.

She tried to pop back to the surface to take a breath, but the branches had tangled with more of her skirts and yanked her short. She couldn't reach the top. Panic began to set in and she desperately ripped at her skirt, trying to tear it with both hands, anything to free herself. The fabric was well-made and didn't budge. Fighting her increasing terror, she tried to snap the limbs that were entangled in her skirts, but the moment her fingers closed around the nearest one, she realized they were too wide and strong to break.

Good God, she couldn't possibly die this way, drowning in a creek that couldn't be more than seven feet deep. Why she'd swum all her life! She and Peter had raced each other back to the shore from far out in the ocean, for heaven's sake. She was no more afraid of water than eating.

But it was no use. She couldn't free herself, and her lungs felt near to bursting from the effort to hold her breath. Frantic, she tried to divest herself of her gown. She'd got the thing nearly off her hips when she felt something large dive into the water next to her.

Strong hands encircled her waist and tugged her hard. Those same hands ripped at her gown, savagely tearing it away from the tree limbs. And then Erienne was free. She popped back to the surface and dragged heavy gulps of air into her starving lungs.

But the effort had tired her, and when she collapsed, it was straight into the arms of none other than Collin Hunt, who had surfaced beside her.

Without saying a word, he hooked his arm under hers and swam swiftly back toward the shore, dragging her with him.

When they made it to the shallow part where they could stand, he gathered her in his arms and carried her onto the bank, where the others had gathered in a frightened little group. She was soaking wet, shivering, clad only in her shift from the waist up.

"What were you thinking?" Collin's voice was laced with

anger and fear as he set her none-too-gently on her feet. "You could have been killed."

Before Erienne had a chance to respond, Anna cleared her throat. "I'll just...take the children back to the house to allow you time to recover, Miss Stone."

"Wait," Collin called. He reached behind him and pulled Mary's doll from where it had apparently been tucked in the waist of his breeches. He held out the doll to the little girl who ran over to grab it with both hands.

"Thank you vewy much, Uncle Collin," Lady Mary said, with a huge smile on her face, before hurrying back to Anna's side.

The nursemaid promptly took both children's hands, turned, and marched doggedly toward the house without looking back.

Erienne sank to the ground and struggled to right her breathing. She had many things to say, but first she needed air, and she wasn't about to waste any of her precious breaths arguing with Collin over why she'd thought she'd be perfectly safe diving into a tiny creek.

She did, however, glance down at herself and notice that her shift was practically see-through, her nipples standing at attention. She plucked at her shift to pull the fabric away from her skin.

Collin had marched over to where they'd made camp only a few minutes earlier and pulled the blanket out from under the basket. He returned to where Erienne sat shivering and wrapped it around her shoulders.

She waited until her teeth stopped chattering. "Th ... thank you," she finally managed.

"You might have died," he repeated, his face etched with a mixture of concern and anger.

Erienne sat for a moment and contemplated that declaration. He was right. She had come close to death this afternoon. It was a frightening thought, but a true one. It immediately drained her of any anger. "I don't know what would have happened if you hadn't come along."

He took a seat on the ground beside her and searched her face. "I'm not trying to garner praise. I was worried sick when I realized you couldn't come up for air. I was watching from down a ways, and came running when—"

Her head snapped up, her eyes seeking his. "You came running to save me?"

"Yes," he admitted, looking positively boyish.

Gratitude washed over her, more powerful than the water of the creek ever could have been. She reached out and pressed a cold hand to his cheek. "Thank you, Collin. I've always considered myself a good swimmer. I suppose I never thought I'd be in danger."

He sat up on his knees and pulled the blanket tighter around her shoulders. "Do you want me to carry you back to the house?"

She tilted her head and considered the offer. "No."

"Would you like me to send for Lucy?"

"No." She pressed her cold, wet nose into the quilt.

He frowned. "Do you want me to walk with you?"

"No."

He cracked a smile. "Would you mind telling me what you'd like to do next, then?"

"This," she said resolutely, before tugging him down atop her, soaking his shirt.

CHAPTER FIFTEEN

The next morning, Collin woke up, rolled over, and groaned. Bloody hell. He'd kissed Erienne yesterday. And the day before. And done more, both times. They'd nearly made love on the creek bed yesterday. God's teeth—she'd had her hand around his cock, and it had taken all the strength in him not to tear off what remained of her clothing and bury himself deep inside of her.

But the woman had nearly died, for Christ's sake. In the end, Collin wasn't so much of a scoundrel that he intended to take advantage of her in her weakened state. Instead, he'd forced himself to pull away from her, wrapped the blanket more snugly around her, gathered the basket, and walked her back to the house, where Anna had already alerted the maids, who were waiting for Erienne with warm blankets and a hot bath.

What the hell was wrong with him? He'd been around Erienne for only two days, and clearly couldn't keep his hands off her. He had no right to appear in her life again and cause havoc. He'd obviously hurt her when he'd left. Even if she hadn't mostly admitted it, he could tell by the acerbic things she'd said at dinner, by the tears in her eyes in the garden, and then there was that brain-rattling slap she'd given him in the library.

He couldn't blame her for hating him. He'd hate himself too if he were in her position. He'd promised her love and marriage and then he'd left her. It didn't matter any longer why he'd done what he'd done. She'd spent the last fourteen years as a governess, a position that was clearly beneath her.

As to why she'd grabbed him and kissed him by the creek bed … that was easily explained. She'd come close to death, and he'd come close to it himself often enough to know that a feeling of euphoria usually followed such an event. Clearly they were still extremely physically attracted to each other. She'd confused her euphoria with passion, that was all. He couldn't blame her for that either, and he certainly hadn't minded. But it hardly meant she was interested in more.

He glanced at the clock on the mantelpiece across from the bed. He'd promised to meet Derek at seven. Collin threw off the sheets and pushed himself out of bed.

WHEN COLLIN ARRIVED at the stables a quarter hour later, his brother was standing by his mount, consulting his timepiece.

"You're late," Derek shot out, his head cocked to the side.

Collin grinned at him. "I'm a gentleman of leisure for the next fortnight, or haven't you heard?"

"Ah, I see. Forgetting your rigid military training so quickly."

"I wish," Collin returned. "Now, didn't you promise me something about showing me the perimeter of the property?" He couldn't wait to get started. A long ride was just what he needed to clear his mind today.

They both mounted their horses and took off at a brisk

trot across the meadow. It wasn't until they were too far away from the house to see it any longer that Derek said, "You all right?"

Collin frowned. "Why wouldn't I be?"

Derek shrugged. "Lucy seems to think something happened between you and Erienne down by the creek yesterday."

Collin's head snapped to face him. "What makes her think that?"

"She said Erienne seemed upset when she returned."

"Erienne almost drowned," Collin ground out.

"Is that all that happened?" Derek countered.

Collin arched a brow at him. "Careful, your grace." It had long been a jest between them for him to call Derek 'your grace.'

"You can't blame us for wondering," Derek replied.

Collin poked out his cheek with his tongue and nodded. "Suffice it to say, I'm thinking of leaving."

Derek lightly kicked his horse's sides to go faster. "Now, that's surprising."

"What do you mean?" Collin called after him.

"I've never known you to run away from anything before. No matter how difficult."

LATER THAT AFTERNOON, Collin strolled through his brother's empty library. He'd already read all the interesting books on military history. He was so desperate for distraction that he'd been looking at tomes on gardening, of all bloody boring things. He'd fully intended to leave this morning, to take himself away from Erienne, to give her the peace she obviously deserved. But then Derek had gone and said the one bloody thing he knew would convince Collin to stay. That Collin wasn't one to run away from difficult things.

And he wasn't, damn it. So why did he want to run from this so much?

Because his emotions were involved. Emotions he barely wanted to acknowledge existed, let alone admit were causing him problems. He'd spent the last fourteen years dedicating himself to work and country, not worrying about things like love and marriage and touching Erienne Stone again. And now because of Lucy and her meddlesome ways, he was trapped in a house with the one woman who made his emotions riot.

He was so lost in thought he didn't hear the door open. When he turned, Erienne was standing near the large leather sofa in the center of the room, the same large leather sofa where he'd pleasured her two nights ago. Bloody hell. *That* thought was not helping.

She hadn't noticed him standing by the bookshelves in the far corner of the room. Instead, she bent to grab a book on the table in front of the sofa. She was wearing a dark gown and an apron. Dressed like a servant. The image of her in her ice-blue gown filled his mind. She should never have to dress like a servant again.

"Good afternoon," he said. Then he wanted to kick himself. *Good afternoon* was a bloody boring thing to say. Besides, the afternoon was not particularly good. It was confusing and tense.

Erienne froze. "Oh," she breathed, hugging the book against her chest. "I just came to fetch a book Mary left here this morning." She glanced down at the cover. "*Cinderella.*"

He folded his hands behind his back and gave a solemn nod. "I've heard of that. Quite popular with the little ones, from what I understand." Another idiotic thing to say. When had he turned into such an idiot?

"It's her favorite." Erienne stood there for a moment, as though casting about for something more to say, then seemed to decide the conversation was over and started for the door.

"Erienne, wait."

She stopped, but didn't turn to him. She stood facing the door, her back ramrod straight.

"Do you want me to leave?" he asked quietly.

She heaved a sigh. "Do you want to go?"

"I don't want to make you uncomfortable."

"If anyone should go, it's me. I'm a servant. You're a part of the family."

"Lucy wouldn't like it if I ran off her new governess."

"Derek wouldn't like it if I ran off his brother," she replied evenly.

Collin chuckled and felt himself relax a little. "Perhaps we're both being unreasonable. What if we agree to a truce? We'll both stay and try to act like civilized human beings to one another. It doesn't need to be difficult."

Erienne turned to face him. "Agreed," she said with the hint of a smile. "It can all be quite simple." She made her way to the desk in the corner and set the book atop it. Then, in a methodical fashion, she pulled a piece of paper out of the top drawer, ripped off a small bit, and grabbed the quill from the inkpot. She scribbled something quickly and waved the paper in the air to dry it. Then, picking up the book again, she walked over to him, handed him the slip, and marched out of the room.

Collin watched her go. The door closed behind her before he allowed his attention to drop to the paper in his hand.

Come to my bedchamber tonight.

CHAPTER SIXTEEN

Erienne paced her bedchamber floor in her shift. It was well after midnight, and she was vibrating with nerves, jumping at any noise. She hadn't seen Collin the rest of the day. She'd remained in the nursery with the children, took her dinner there with Anna, and then retired early, not long after the children went to sleep.

Had she made an awful mistake giving that note to Collin? She hadn't stayed to see his reaction, but for all she knew, he thought it was completely inappropriate. Or perhaps he'd been tempted, but had no intention of actually arriving at her door tonight. Hadn't he just finished telling her they could both act like civilized human beings around each other? Hadn't he been the one to stop what had happened at the creek? The truth was she didn't want to act like a civilized human being around him. She hadn't wanted to stop what happened at the creek. She wanted to rip off the man's clothes and make love to him all night.

She'd spent last night tossing and turning, and finally decided what she wanted: one night with Collin. Perhaps if they spent the night together, she would be able to forget about him once and for all. Perhaps she'd be able to banish him from her thoughts and heart for good.

She'd remained a virgin all these years. Didn't she deserve one night of passion? It wasn't as if she was saving herself for marriage. That dream had vanished long ago. On the contrary, she intended to live the rest of her life as a spinster and a governess. What did her virginity matter any longer? She might as well give it to the man to whom it had belonged all along. The only man she'd ever loved.

A soft knock on the door made her jump. She pressed a hand to her pounding heart and forced herself to slowly cross the room and open it, her bare feet sliding along the thick rug.

When she swung open the door, Collin stood there, a small bouquet of purple and white wildflowers in his fist. She couldn't help her smile.

"I didn't think you'd come," she breathed.

"I've yet to miss a challenge."

She stood back to allow him to enter the room. "I suppose that's true," she told him, "but I wasn't certain you'd want to participate in this one."

She shut the door behind him, took the flowers from his hand, and pressed them to her nose. Their soft, cool petals tickled her, their scent fresh and sweet. "Thank you."

Collin reached out and traced a fingertip along her cheek. "Why wouldn't I come, Erienne?"

She took a deep breath and forced herself to meet his eyes. "We aren't children anymore. I invited you here to do more than just kiss me."

His eyes flashed green fire. "And I accepted for the same purpose."

She made her way over to the bed and laid the flowers on

91

the nightstand. Then, sensing he had more to say, she turned to look at him.

"I thought ..." He shook his head and seemed to gather his thoughts. "At the creek, I thought you were overcome by what had happened. Nearly drowning, I mean."

"I was," she agreed, "but that didn't mean I didn't want you. I've always wanted you."

At her soft admission, he seemed to melt a little. His defenses. All the armor hiding his emotions. Pain crossed his features and he closed his eyes and drew in a breath. When he opened them, he stalked across the room to meet her and pulled her into his arms. "Are you certain this is what you want, Erienne?"

"I've never been more certain." Of course, she had no intention of telling him this was all she wanted. One night. One night to remember forever. "Kiss me," she breathed.

He lowered his mouth to hers and kissed her softly at first. But then the passion too long suppressed surged between them, and he claimed her lips with a possessiveness that brought her to her toes.

Her arms slid around his neck, and he wasted no time pulling off her shift in a single, upward sweep that left her hair wild and curling around her face and shoulders.

Together, they worked with frantic haste to divest Collin of his clothing. He stopped momentarily to sit on the edge of the mattress and shuck his boots, which hit the floor none-too-gently, thudding out his intentions.

When at last they were both naked—him unashamed, his gaze hungrily skimming every inch of her, and Erienne shivering with part shyness, part delight and trepidation—he drew her down onto the mattress, where they could gaze at each other in wonder and revel in the feel of each other's naked skin.

"You're beautiful." She traced a trembling finger along the fine musculature of his chest.

He chuckled. "I believe that's what I'm supposed to say to you." His gaze darkened as it flickered down her body. "You are, by the way, beyond beautiful."

He lowered himself atop her. His dark head moved to her nipple, and he bit it gently and let his tongue toy with it before sucking it into the sweet heat of his mouth. She moaned and arched her back. "Collin," she whispered.

When she was squirming with delight, he shifted his attention lower, a slow, sinful trajectory, pausing at her belly to shower kisses on the tender skin and dip his tongue into her navel, which seemed as explicit an act as any Erienne had shared with him before tonight.

Until Collin's mouth found the aching place between her legs.

She stared down at him in a haze of lust, not entirely certain what he was doing, only that it involved his lips, his tongue … and she never wanted him to stop.

His soft hair brushed her inner thighs as he gently nudged and probed with his tongue to find that perfect spot. When she let out a gasp, she felt him smile against her flesh, and then his insistent tongue wreaked havoc on her senses, the building pleasure sending her body to seek and follow the hot touch of his mouth.

"You taste so sweet, Erienne," he breathed against her skin.

She sank her fingers into his hair, her thighs tensing on either side of his head. She was mindless. Her head thrashed fitfully against the pillow, her legs straining more with each relentless stroke of his tongue.

Erienne had squeezed her eyes closed, grasping at every wild sensation, but her lashes lifted the instant she felt the slow slide of his finger inside her—first a tentative probing, and then, gradually, a sinuous rhythm, in and out, gliding against her wetness. Never did his tongue falter in its own dance on her, and suddenly the pleasure was too great, and her consciousness took flight in a riot of swirls and colors as her body shuddered beneath his sensual assault, utterly separate from her will.

When she came back to herself again, Collin's hand was tenderly stroking her hair, his lips whispering against her ear things she never thought she'd hear him say again. Things about how much he cherished and wanted her, how much he'd missed her, and how badly he wanted to bury himself inside her.

He'd given her indescribable pleasure twice now, some kind of otherworldly miracle she hadn't even known her body was capable of experiencing. But she wasn't doing this solely for herself. He'd also been denied the sensual union they'd both wanted all these years.

She smiled and a surge of feminine power seized her as she leaned up on one elbow and pressed him back against the mattress. Then she slowly moved atop him, never breaking contact with his hot gaze. To her surprise, he capitulated, stretching his arms above his head, giving himself over to her completely. She kissed him deeply, enough to draw the breath from him. Then she moved down his body, the same path of delight and promise as he had hers, showering kisses on his taut abdomen until she reached the apex of his thighs. His long, hard manhood stood out from the dark hair there. She wrapped her fist around it just as she'd done at the creek.

He groaned and closed his eyes. "Erienne."

She felt drunk with the power her touch had over him. They'd never been like this before. Naked, carefree, able to do whatever they wanted to each other, however they wanted to do it. She intended to take full advantage of this freedom.

She lowered herself until her mouth hovered over his member. Then her tongue darted out to lick the tip. His big, strong body shuddered. She smiled to herself.

She touched her tongue to the tip again, but this time, she slid her mouth over it too, sucked a little, and instantly realized she'd discovered something astonishing and perhaps primal. His body gave a wild buck and shiver, a helpless sound rumbling in his throat.

Which had to mean that he'd liked it.

"Tell me what to do to you, Collin," she whispered fervently, letting his hot, hard flesh slip from her lips to slide along her cheek. "Tell me what you want."

COLLIN FLICKED open his eyes and stared down at Erienne. He'd never felt such overwhelming desire. His dreams had never been this good. Erienne was in bed with him, nude and wanting him. No one would stop them. She'd asked him to show her what he wanted. *That* was a dream come true.

He didn't trust himself to speak, so he merely took her hand and folded her fingers around his cock. Those cool, smooth, graceful fingers. Their touch nearly set him off like an untried lad. He swallowed and refocused, then guided her touch into a gentle slide, up and down.

Erienne caught on quickly, and soon his guiding hand fell away to clench itself into a fist at his side, his entire body poised on the edge of a climax, controlled only by his will to revel in having her and this moment.

And all the while, she watched her own ministrations in wide-eyed wonder, a smile of joy and marvel on her lips, as though finally awakened to the intimate gifts she could offer.

When his breath tore in ragged pants from his throat and his hips were pushing to meet every downward slip of her

VALERIE BOWMAN

hand, he grabbed her fingers and pulled them away. But she'd already learned what he liked, and she quickly swept in to substitute her mouth, sucking him, resuming the devastating caress of a moment before with her lips, tongue, and even the slight graze of her teeth.

Collin clutched the pillow on either side of his head and bit the inside of his cheek hard, anything to keep from coming. He wanted to make love to her the right way, to feel her body quicken again, to bring her to climax again, to make her cry out his name. But he couldn't summon the will to pull her mouth away from his aching cock.

Ah, God. Just one moment more. Just one sweet moment more. Or two.

Erienne clenched his cock in her fist and dragged her lips up and down the length, her tongue mapping the ridges and texture of him. When she took the tip into her mouth again, as deeply as she could, his hips arched off the mattress and nearly tumbled her off the bed.

"Jesus," he groaned, and with that, he broke the spell, grasped her around the waist and drew her fully atop him, at last regaining control.

They rolled on the mattress until she was beneath him again, and he settled in the cradle between her legs.

"I want you," he said, kissing her cheek, her ear, her neck.

"I want you too," she breathed, tilting her head back to grant him better access to her tender skin.

Collin lifted on one knee, nudged her thighs farther apart, and positioned himself above her, his cock probing her wet heat. "Are you certain, Erienne?"

"Yes," she whispered. "Take me."

He closed his eyes, and without preamble slid slowly but determinedly into her wet warmth.

Halfway, he paused, reading the stutter of her exhalations against his ear, counting the wild hammer of her heartbeats against his own chest. He let his lips wander over her cheek, her mouth, her forehead.

Comforting. Waiting.

Only when her fingertips, which had been digging hard into the muscles of his back, relaxed ever so slightly, did he give a last firm thrust and sink to the hilt within her.

He lifted his head to read her features. "Did it hurt?" he asked softly.

She rolled her eyes thoughtfully, as though considering. "Just a pinch." Then she smiled.

That humor faded into pleasure-pain when he began to move inside her. She moaned, her lashes slid closed, and soon her limbs encircled him, holding him closer as his hips levered against hers, pushing, pressing, arching against her.

It took every ounce of discipline not to come, but he was determined to know the rise and quake of her body in climax yet again. His hand slid between them and he found the flashpoint of her pleasure with a single fingertip, drawing circles, drawing her toward ecstasy, even as he balanced on the edge of his own completion.

At last—and far more quickly than he could have guessed it could happen—Erienne's hands clenched against his shoulders and she arched beneath him. Her entire body went rigid, her ragged pants momentarily silent, and then she came in a rush, shuddered wildly, and cried his name against her ear.

Only when her limbs slackened around him did he let his body drive itself inside her as it sought by nature, pumping into her again and again, until he too, was swept into sweet oblivion.

They lay like the dead for a long minute, each struggling to regain breath, each loath to draw apart, though perspiration made their skin slick and sticky, and Collin's arm had gone numb beneath Erienne's back.

At last she shifted a little beneath him, and he slipped to

the side and instantly regained their embrace, wrapped his arms around her, and rested his head in the fragrant crook of her neck. A huge, exhausted sigh escaped both of them simultaneously, one of satiation, a release of years of wanting and tension and grief and confusion. It was all behind them now. He never wanted to let her go again.

He would tell her in the morning.

CHAPTER SEVENTEEN

One single, piercing band of sunlight streamed through the window, hitting Collin in the eye and waking him. He stretched and yawned, and then ... Damn. He was still in Erienne's bed, and it was morning. He would have to leave immediately and be careful about it. He quickly rolled over to reach for her ... and found the space beside him empty and cold.

He pushed himself up and frowned. Where was she? Had she gone to be with the children? It wasn't that late, was it? He scrubbed a hand over his face, squinting to see the clock on the mantelpiece. It was barely after six. Surely she wasn't with the children at this hour. Besides, if she'd gone to be with them, why hadn't she wakened him and asked him to leave?

A piece of paper on the nightstand caught his eye. It was folded. Edging himself up against the headboard, he grabbed the paper and scanned it. A smaller bit of paper floated out to land on the coverlet. He ignored it for the moment.

C,

*I had to go. I cannot allow your lovely sister-in-law to do
more for me than she already has. I never should have come
here in the first place. Last night was beautiful, and I'll
cherish it forever. I hope you will too.
E*

He cursed under his breath. Damn. Damn. Damn. She'd
gone. But why? He'd thought she wanted him. He'd thought
she'd changed her mind.

He picked up the tiny piece of paper on the coverlet. *Let
me go.*

Bloody hell. He clenched his jaw. Apparently, he'd
thought wrong.

～

ONE HOUR LATER, Collin was cleaned, dressed, and sitting in
the breakfast room with Derek. Of course, he couldn't let on
that he knew Erienne was gone, but it was all he could think
about. He hadn't said more than two words to his brother
since they'd begun their meal.

Why had she left? He'd assumed she wanted more than
just a night with him. How could he have been so wrong? He
was a bloody spy, for Christ's sake. Trained to pick up on the
tiniest fluctuations in people's voice and mannerisms, their
slightest hesitations, their smallest clues. How the hell had he
completely misread the situation with Erienne?

But damn it. He already knew. He'd always misread
Erienne because the depth of his feelings for her clouded his
judgment.

Lucy came bustling into the room. "Miss Stone is gone."
Her voice held a mixture of anger, frustration, and a hint of
accusation.

"What?" Derek frowned.

Lucy crossed her arms over her chest. "Erienne left a note under my bedchamber door saying she never should have accepted this position, and that she was awfully sorry but she was heading back to London. Apparently, one of the groomsmen took her to the coaching station early this morning."

Lucy and Derek both looked at Collin, who continued to shove the eggs around his plate in silence.

"You wouldn't happen to know anything about why she left, would you, Collin?" Lucy finally asked, her hands on her hips.

"Should I?" he drawled, making eye contact with his sister-in-law.

"I'd be surprised if you didn't," she replied, arching a brow.

Collin clenched his jaw and tossed down his fork. "Perhaps Erienne was right. Perhaps she never *should* have accepted this position in the first place." He knew his words sounded cruel and callous, but at the moment he didn't care. He was bloody furious with Erienne for leaving without telling him she intended to go. He'd at least spoken to her in person when he'd given her up all those years ago. They weren't children any longer. This was serious.

"What did you say to upset her?" Lucy demanded.

"Why do you assume she left because of me?" Collin snapped.

"Enough." Derek's voice shot through the room like a crack of thunder. "I think we all can agree this situation was fraught from the start. I'm sorry if any of us caused Miss Stone pain."

"Too late for that," Lucy mumbled.

Collin narrowed his eyes. "What's that supposed to mean?"

She tossed a hand in the air, a gesture of utter impatience.

"Erienne is gone, Collin. Aren't you going to do something about it?"

"Would you like me to review the letters from the other governess applicants?" Collin countered.

Lucy turned on her heel and stalked from the room. "Men!" she called as she went. "You can all be so exasperatingly obtuse!"

CHAPTER EIGHTEEN

Erienne glanced around the sad little flat that a perfectly pleasant woman named Mrs. Cartwright had just finished showing her. The tour hadn't taken long—the flat consisted of only one room. It contained a bed with a lumpy-looking mattress and two doubtfully clean pillows. Two rickety chairs and a small, equally rickety table. A tiny kitchen with a stove that looked questionable at best, and a ramshackle wardrobe pushed against the far wall that sat askew, one of its wooden legs missing.

The space was all Erienne could afford with her savings from her position with the Hilltops. She'd sent the rest of her money home for Peter, and she hadn't stayed with Derek and Lucy long enough to collect wages. After leaving them so suddenly, she didn't deserve either their money or their reference.

Erienne glanced around the room again. It was a far cry from her gorgeous suite at Huntingdon, and it smelled like a mixture of dust and mold. Tears burned the backs of her eyes, but she blinked them away. "I'll take it," she informed Mrs. Cartwright. The woman smiled and nodded.

Erienne handed the older woman the money for one week's rent, and Mrs. Cartwright handed her the key to her dubious new home.

"I'll just ask the coachman ta bring up yer trunk then," the woman said as she headed for the door.

All Erienne could do was nod. "Thank you," she finally managed.

The door closed behind Mrs. Cartwright, and Erienne wrapped her arms over her middle. She'd felt empty and awful the entire ride back to London, and she wasn't feeling any better now that she'd secured lodging for the night.

She would miss little Lady Mary and cute little Ralph. Hopefully Anna wasn't too put out by her leaving so suddenly, or for that matter, Lucy. Lucy had been so kind to her. The duchess fancied herself a matchmaker. She'd done her best to bring Erienne and Collin back together—but sometimes things were better left in the past. It was a difficult lesson, one that Erienne was just beginning to learn.

Leaving had been the right thing to do. At least she'd decided that much on her long, bumpy ride back from the countryside. She was certain she'd made the correct choice. So why did she feel so ... sad? She'd had to leave. Because she knew, without a doubt, that Collin would let her go again. Just as he had the first time, without any attempt to stop her, and ultimately that was why they shouldn't be together. True love didn't let go. And Collin had let go. Twice now, by her count.

His work had been more important to him than she was the first time. Perhaps his pride was what would keep him away this time, but it didn't matter the reason. Whatever his excuse, the result was the same. Collin didn't love her enough to fight for her, and he never had. It was sad and unfortunate, but it was true.

She hadn't left to test him. Never that. She'd left because

she knew in her bones that she never should have accepted the position as governess in Lucy and Derek's house in the first place. She'd known it was wrong and she'd taken it regardless, out of greed for the wages she'd been promised, but even more, hoping to catch a glimpse of Collin or at least hear some news.

Now she'd done far more than that.

She'd left for another reason as well. She never in a thousand years wanted Collin to think she'd spent the night with him because she expected more from him than that. There was no better way to make it clear. She hadn't been attempting to force an offer from him or to appeal to his sense of guilt or duty. She wanted him as a woman wants a man, and she'd been telling the truth when she wrote him the good-bye letter telling him she'd never forget last night. She would cherish the memory forever. It was all she'd have of him for the rest of her life.

Now she needed to get about the business of once again forgetting the past and moving on with the future, her maxim. Even if it would be twice as difficult this time around.

First things first. Once she was settled here, she'd pay a visit to Mrs. Griggs and attempt to explain the situation in person. Perhaps if Erienne was convincing, her employer might take pity on her for leaving Huntingdon and send her for an interview at another house.

She would get through this minute by minute, hour by hour, day by day, but no matter what, she wouldn't think of Collin Hunt. She would not.

And she refused to have any regrets.

CHAPTER NINETEEN

Darkness had fallen when a knock on the door to her flat startled Erienne. She'd started off trying to unpack her trunk, but instead she'd been staring blindly into the rickety wardrobe, lost in thought. She shook herself, made her way over to the door, and called, "Who is it?"

London could be a dangerous place for a lone female, and although she was a confirmed spinster and traveled without a maid, she wasn't about to open the door to just anyone, especially at night.

"It's Lucy Hunt. May I come in?"

Erienne let out a startled gasp and then immediately clapped her hands over her mouth, praying the duchess hadn't heard the noise.

Drat. She hated to allow a woman as grand as the Duchess of Claringdon to see the pathetic flat she'd taken. Of course, if Lucy had made it this far into the building, no doubt she already had a good guess as to how wretched the interior would be.

Erienne immediately unlocked the door and swung it open.

There stood the duchess, in her fine kid boots and traveling coat, wearing an expression that could only be described as both guilty and regretful. "May I come in?" she asked softly.

"Of course."

Erienne moved aside and Lucy stepped past her into the space. She didn't betray her thoughts as to the look of the place, but Erienne's cheeks heated with shame nonetheless. "Your grace—"

"Now, none of that," the duchess replied. "I asked you to call me Lucy, and I expect you always to call me Lucy."

"Very well. Lucy." Erienne motioned to the small table and chairs, the only place to sit. Without hesitation, Lucy strolled over and took a seat as though they were visiting in the finest salon. The duchess beckoned to Erienne to take the seat beside her.

Erienne did so while making a helpless gesture. "I'd offer to take your coat and hat and provide tea, but—"

"No need. I don't intend to stay long."

Erienne took a deep breath. "I'm sorry you felt you had to come all the way from the country to find me. I left a note."

"I read it," Lucy replied. "I tracked you down by asking the coachman at the posting house where you'd gone."

Erienne nodded. "I'm sorry, Lucy. Truly I am. I just couldn't—"

"Dear, it is I who owes you an apology. As my husband likes to point out, at times I can be a bit … overzealous in my quest to ensure true love has its chance." She leaned forward to capture Erienne's gaze. "I fear, in this case, I failed you."

A small part of Erienne, the one that had foolishly hoped Lucy had come to say Collin was beside himself and wanted her back, died a quick death within her soul. "I knew it was a mistake to take the position, and I did so out of greed. It's entirely my fault."

"It wasn't greed, though, was it, dear? I cannot believe you took the position only because of the pay." She peered at Erienne with those knowing, different-colored eyes.

Erienne bit her lip. "I'd be lying if I didn't admit that I'd wanted to learn more about Collin."

"To see him?" Lucy prompted.

"Eventually. I never expected it to happen so quickly, however. It was too much. I'm afraid I was too weak."

Lucy reached across the small table and squeezed her hand. "Nonsense, Erienne. From what I've seen, you're one of the strongest women I've ever known. You left your home and a life of comfort to take a position as a servant rather than compromise on true love. I don't know many women who would have done that."

Erienne stared unseeing at the dusty wooden floorboards. "I never saw it that way."

"Of course you didn't, dear. Strong people rarely recognize their own strength. But I see it. I see it and I admire you for it."

Tears burned Erienne's eyes. "I hope you'll be able to forgive me. I'm certain you'll find another governess quickly. One far more suitable than I ever was."

Lucy pulled her reticule atop her lap, opened it, and withdrew a folded sheet of vellum. She handed it to Erienne. "This is a character reference, signed by both Derek and myself. I'd hate for my pestering you to take the position with us to cause you trouble with Mrs. Griggs. I intend to visit her myself tomorrow morning, speak highly of you, and ensure you're given every opportunity to interview for the next suitable position that becomes available."

Erienne pressed her lips together. "Thank you, your—er, Lucy. That is far more generous than I deserve."

The duchess stood and stepped toward the door. "You deserve much more than you've got, Erienne. And if my brother-in-law wasn't such a fool, you'd get it."

Erienne tried to withhold the instant response that sprang to her lips, but they had a mind of their own. "How is ... he?" Why, *why* couldn't she stop caring about him? Stop wondering about him?

Lucy turned to her, sympathy shining in her eyes. "I don't know what happened between the two of you, Erienne, either all those years ago or over the last few days, but I do know that one drunken night not too, too long ago, Collin told me about you, and I knew without a doubt he loved you desperately."

Tears slid down Erienne's cheeks. She dashed them away with the backs of her hands. Lucy had said *loved*. The word was in the past tense.

"I hope you know that's the only reason I attempted to meddle in your affairs," the duchess continued. "I truly did it for the very best of reasons."

Erienne heaved a sigh. She pulled a handkerchief from her pocket and dabbed at her eyes. "I know you did, Lucy. I know."

Lucy turned back toward the door. "I should go. The coach is waiting, and I need to be awake early to visit Mrs. Griggs before I return to Huntingdon."

"Thank you for coming all this way and giving me the reference," Erienne said, rising to follow her to the threshold.

"You're more than welcome, dear." And with that, the duchess was gone.

CHAPTER TWENTY

Collin was fishing in the creek the next morning when Derek caught up to him. He'd brought his pole and a bucket of bait. As youths, the brothers had spent countless hours silently fishing side-by-side. Derek's appearance felt strangely like old times.

Derek baited his hook and slung his line into the water. "Catch anything?"

"Not yet," Collin replied.

"Pity."

It was an old jest between them. As children, whenever their mother had come looking for them, asking if they'd caught anything, and they said no, she'd respond with, "Pity." As children, it had made them laugh. Neither of them laughed today.

Several silent minutes passed before Collin finally asked, "Lucy went to London yesterday?"

"Yes. She'll be back this evening."

"She went to see Erienne?"

Derek stared out across the lake. "She wanted to make

certain Erienne has a decent reference. Lucy blames herself for all of this."

Collin flashed him a rueful glance. "Funny. I could have sworn she blamed me."

A half-smile appeared on Derek's lips. "She blames you for being an obtuse male."

"Guilty as charged, I suppose."

Derek continued to stare out across the water. "I would never ask this, of course, because I am a man and we don't ask such things of other men, but if Lucy were here, she would want to know why you let Erienne go."

"I didn't *let* her go. She left me … again." Collin's voice was cold as ice, even to his own ears.

"She didn't leave you the first time, did she?" his brother asked. "You told her you wouldn't marry her."

He frowned at Derek. "How did you—?"

"Lucy told me you mentioned Erienne to her once when you were in your cups. I think you're forgetting another time you were in your cups," Derek added, finally shifting his attention from the water to Collin's face. "One night, fourteen years ago, we'd both come home on leave together. You'd been out for a while that afternoon, and we went to the pub in town. You drank more that night than I've ever seen you drink. And you told me what happened with Erienne."

Collin cursed under his breath. "Leaving her was the bloody most painful thing I've ever done."

"I understand, believe me. I also understand what it feels like to think you're not good enough." He set down his pole and scooped up a stone from the creek bed. "After I was made a duke, it took a great deal of time before I felt anywhere near comfortable around the aristocracy. Lucy was the only one I felt right with for a long time. And that's because she's so unconventional."

Collin blew out a breath. "What are you trying to say, Derek?"

"I'm saying that you and I are the same. We came from nothing, and we've felt as if we deserve nothing because of it. But that's not true. You've made yourself the man you are today, Collin, and you deserve everything good in life. Including love."

Collin hung his head. "You don't understand. She's always been too good for me."

"She's always loved you. She sees who you are, not where you came from."

Collin clenched his jaw so tightly it hurt. "But what if I don't know how to be good enough for her?"

"You're already good enough. You always have been. That's what it means to be loved." Derek clapped his brother on the shoulder. "What do you want, Collin? For once in your life, think about your own desire, your own pleasure, not what's expected of you, not what you think you don't deserve."

Collin shook his head and tried to retort, to douse the emotion roiling in the air, but the words caught on the lump that had formed in his throat.

"You've spent your entire life denying yourself everything," his brother said more gently. "You're more interested in your paperwork than your feelings. Believe me, I understand, but when you're on your deathbed one day ..." Derek pitched the stone at the water, watched it skip and sink, then he looked at Collin again, hard. "Paperwork is cold comfort, Coll. Ask yourself, for once ... what do *you* truly want?"

CHAPTER TWENTY-ONE

Exactly one sennight later, Erienne sat in the Countess of Marsden's drawing room. The countess had four children ranging in age from six months to six years, and she was looking for a suitable governess. Mrs. Griggs, having spoken at length with the Duchess of Claringdon, had seen fit to send Erienne to this interview, and Erienne was hoping against hope she'd be offered the position. She'd spent her last shilling on this week's rent, and she'd just received a letter from home indicating that Peter had taken a turn for the worse.

"Your references are impeccable," Lady Marsden said. "You speak fluent French and—"

The door to the countess's drawing room flew open and Collin Hunt came striding in, looking handsome and dashing in his uniform, his rows of medals shining in the sunlight that streamed through the windows.

Well.

For an instant, no one moved. Then Erienne gulped and hid an involuntary smile.

"What is the meaning of this?" Lady Marsden glanced

around as if someone might explain to her why a strange man had just burst into her drawing room.

The butler came running in behind Collin. "My apologies, my lady," the man said, looking as if he'd never been so affronted in his life. "I tried to stop him, but this soldier insisted upon seeing ... Miss Stone."

"Miss Stone?" the countess repeated, clutching at her pearls. She turned to Erienne and stared at her. "Why is the army after you?"

Erienne could only stare at Collin. "What are you doing here?"

He marched over to her and dropped to one knee in front of the settee where she sat. Then, as though he and Erienne were the only people in the room, he took both of her hands in his and gazed deeply into her eyes. "I'm sorry to interrupt you like this, but I couldn't wait another moment to tell you that I love you madly and cannot live my life without you. Will you marry me, Erienne Stone?"

The countess rapidly fanned herself while the butler looked aghast.

Tears of joy and repressed grief burned her eyes. "Do you mean it, Collin? You're not here out of guilt?" She searched his handsome face for even the faintest flicker of something amiss.

"Never." He shook his head.

"Duty?" she asked next.

"Absolutely not." He shook his head again.

"Because Lucy sent you?" she finally asked.

Collin's bark of laughter filled the room. "I've never done anything Lucy told me to before, and I've no intention to begin now. I'm here because we're meant for each other, and always have been. I'll never let you go again."

Erienne laughed. Then she cried. Then she jumped up, threw herself into his arms, and wrapped her arms around his neck. "Yes, Collin Hunt, I'll marry you. I'll marry you whenever you like."

"Excellent." He slid an arm beneath her legs, lifted her, and marched toward the door.

"Miss Stone?" the forgotten countess called from her perch on the settee, waving her handkerchief in the air. "Does this mean you're no longer interested in the position as governess?"

"That's right, Lady Marsden," Erienne replied over Collin's shoulder, torn between tears and laughter. "I've changed my plans. I'm now set to wed General Collin Hunt, high-ranking official in the Home Office, and the only man I've ever loved."

"I see," Lady Marsden called as the newly betrothed couple made their way into the foyer. "Perhaps you should let Mrs. Griggs know?"

Erienne and Collin both laughed uproariously as he carried her out the front door, down the steps to the street, and to his waiting coach. He helped her inside and pulled himself up after her. Once the coach door was closed behind them, he tugged her into his arms and kissed her until she couldn't breathe, which was fine because she'd always secretly imagined she could survive on his kisses alone.

"You came for me," Erienne murmured after the kiss ended.

"Just righting a wrong I made fourteen years ago," he replied with a tender smile.

"What took you so long?"

"I've been a fool," he said, lifting her hand to his lips, "but I intend to make up for it with all due haste."

She watched, hypnotized, as his tender kiss brushed across her knuckles. Then she swallowed and said, "You thought I was married in Shropsbury, didn't you?"

Collin gave a solemn nod. "Your mother told me you were."

"What?" Horror washed over her. How could her mother spin such a lie, and one that would destroy her own daughter's future for so very long?

"I came for you that Christmas," Collin said. "The Christmas after you left. Your mother told me you'd married a viscount and moved to Shropsbury."

Erienne pressed a hand to her throat, tears welling anew on her lashes at the thought of him, so young and hopeful, arriving at her family home and meeting with the impenetrable brick wall of righteousness that was her mother. "That's horrible. I never knew."

"At the time, I assumed it was for the best. I thought I wasn't good enough for you, Air. I still think that. But I intend to spend the rest of my life attempting to become good enough."

She wrapped her arms around his neck again. "You only have to be yourself, darling."

"Yes, well, as to that. I intend to stop working so much and take a great many more holidays."

She laughed as he nuzzled her neck. "Is that so?"

"Yes," he said lightly, and with complete certainty. "I find I'm quite preoccupied with my new pastime."

"Which is?" She leaned her head back against the velvet squabs of the coach and closed her eyes.

"Making love to my beautiful wife."

"Hmm. I like the sound of that."

"Lord Treadway is just going to have to manage without me."

"He'll be fine," Erienne replied.

"I agree," Collin declared, pushing the sleeves of her gown over her arms to kiss the tops of her breasts.

"Are you going to make love to me in a carriage of all places?" she asked, slightly scandalized.

He arched a brow. "Any objections?"

"None whatsoever," she said with a laugh. "Carry on, General."

CHAPTER TWENTY-TWO

The wedding took place exactly four weeks later, after the banns had been read in Brighton. Erienne's parents both attended, even though she'd had strong words with her mother for her deception all those years ago. Her parents were quite willing to accept Collin into their family now that he was a general, a highly valued spy, and an official at the Home Office. Not to mention he was wealthy. He'd set about paying all of the bills for Peter's surgery; and had even given her father money to perform some much needed restorations to their family home. Derek sent a virtual army of craftsmen to complete the work. Seemed the Hunt boys from the small cottage on the wrong side of town were the pride of Brighton these days.

Little Lady Mary and Lord Ralph were dressed in finery for the wedding, and Lucy hugged both the bride and groom an inordinate amount of times. "I must admit," she told them after the ceremony, "you two frightened me more than any couple in the history of my matchmaking endeavors."

"Yes, well, it seems we're going to be in need of a new governess ... again," Derek said with a sigh.

Lucy smiled and patted her husband's arm. "Don't worry. I kept all the letters from Mrs. Griggs."

Derek's brows shot up. "That confident, were you, that these two would get back together?"

"I'd be lying if I said I wasn't," Lucy replied with a nonchalant shrug.

Her arm resting comfortably in Collin's, Erienne leaned in and confided to her friend, "Your unswayable romantic convictions are nothing short of admirable, dear Lucy."

"Indeed." Collin added dryly, but then shared a gentle smile with his bride.

Derek looked less certain. "Very well, Lucy, but next time, can you please find a governess who is already married, or perhaps a nice widow?"

"I can make no promises." Lucy winked at him.

"Seriously, Lucy, when *will* you stop matchmaking?" Collin asked.

Lucy tapped a finger against her cheek. "I suppose I'll die eventually. Perhaps at that time I'll consider retirement. Until then ... my friend Delilah Montebank has made her debut, and hers shall be the match of the century."

ALSO BY VALERIE BOWMAN

Playful Brides

The Unexpected Duchess (Book 1)

The Accidental Countess (Book 2)

The Unlikely Lady (Book 3)

The Irresistible Rogue (Book 4)

The Unforgettable Hero (Book 4.5)

The Untamed Earl (Book 5)

The Legendary Lord (Book 6)

Never Trust a Pirate (Book 7)

The Right Kind of Rogue (Book 8)

A Duke Like No Other (Book 9)

Kiss Me At Christmas (Book 10)

Mr. Hunt, I Presume (Book 10.5)

No Other Duke But You (Book 11)

Secret Brides

Secrets of a Wedding Night (Book 1)

A Secret Proposal (Book 1.5)

Secrets of a Runaway Bride (Book 2)

A Secret Affair (Book 2.5)

Secrets of a Scandalous Marriage (Book 3)

It Happened Under the Mistletoe (Book 3.5)

AUTHOR'S NOTE

Thank you for reading *Mr. Hunt, I Presume.* I hope you enjoyed Erienne and Collin's story.

Second-chance romance is my absolute favorite and this little book flew off my fingertips in a week's time.

I'd love to keep in touch.

- Visit my website for information about upcoming books, excerpts, and to sign up for my email newsletter: www.ValerieBowmanBooks.com or at www.ValerieBowmanBooks.com/subscribe.
- Join me on Facebook: http://Facebook.com/ValerieBowmanAuthor.
- Follow me on Twitter at @ValerieGBowman, https://twitter.com/ValerieGBowman
- Reviews help other readers find books. I appreciate all reviews, whether positive or negative. Thank you so much for considering it!

ABOUT THE AUTHOR

Valerie Bowman grew up in Illinois with six sisters (she's number seven) an a huge supply of historical romance novels. After a cold and snowy stint earning a degree in English with a minor in history at Smith College, she moved to Florida the first chance she got. Valerie now lives in Jacksonville with her family including her two rascally dogs. When she's not writing, she keeps busy reading, traveling, or vacillating between watching crazy reality TV and PBS.

Valerie loves to hear from readers. Find her on the web at www.ValerieBowmanBooks.com.

- facebook.com/ValerieBowmanAuthor
- twitter.com/ValerieGBowman
- instagram.com/ValerieGBowman
- goodreads.com/Valerie_Bowman
- pinterest.com/ValerieGBowman
- bookbub.com/authors/valerie-bowman

COMING SOON

Look for the next novel in the Playful Brides Series by
Valerie Bowman.

No Other Duke But You

Coming May 2019 from St. Martin's Paperbacks
turn the page to read an excerpt

A DUKE LIKE NO OTHER - CHAPTER ONE

London, June 1827

Twenty-two-year-old Lady Delilah Montebank peered around the corner of the servants' staircase while her friends smuggled a small potted tree, an armload of paper moss, and a set of fake donkey ears down the back steps of her mother's town house.

"*J'adore* the donkey ears," she whispered, glancing over her shoulder to check for witnesses. Her chin brushed against the ruffles of her pink gown. "Shh. We cannot let Mother hear."

Her friends, Owen Monroe, the Earl of Moreland, Christian Forester, Viscount Berkeley, and Derek Hunt, the Duke of Claringdon, all dutifully slipped out the back door, their arms full, without making a sound.

"*Merci beaucoup,*" she whispered to Derek, as his boots crunched the gravel on the way to his coach. "Please tell Lucy I'll see her tomorrow." She waved at the duke.

Derek inclined his head by way of reply.

Delilah turned and let out a deep breath. She'd been skittish all morning, hoping her mother wouldn't find her friends smuggling the decorations for the play out of her bedchamber. But Mother hadn't discovered them. Job well done.

Delilah was about to close the door behind her when a small red squirrel dashed inside. The squirrel took off down the corridor toward the front of the house.

Delilah winced. She may have met this squirrel before. She *may* have fed it, which meant she may be responsible for its entrance into her home. And if Mother or Cook saw it first, the poor little animal would be doomed.

Delilah hiked up her skirts and took off after the squirrel. The rodent dashed back and forth down the corridor, leaping left and right, heading directly for the front of the house as if he knew the layout. Mother was in the front drawing room receiving visitors. The door to the gold salon was open. She might see the squirrel dash past. Of course, Delilah knew this because she'd thoroughly researched her mother's whereabouts before telling her friends to proceed with smuggling things out the back door.

The squirrel was already in the foyer by the time Delilah caught up to it. It paused and looked about. Delilah paused too, holding her breath. She stood panting and waiting, her skirts still hiked above her stockinged ankles. Mother's voice drifted from the salon. Delilah swallowed, her eyes darting to the side.

The squirrel dashed across the marble floor and ran under a rosewood table, the same rosewood table that housed the expensive crystal bowl in which visitors left their calling cards. The same crystal bowl Mother was excessively proud of.

Mother's voiced drifted from the salon again. She was saying good-bye to someone, which meant she was about to emerge from the room. Delilah didn't have much time. She expelled a breath and eyed the squirrel warily. It sat under the table, sniffing the air and swishing its bushy tail. Delilah had no choice. Time was of the essence. She dove for the squirrel, catching her slipper in the hem of her skirt and ripping it, upending the table, and smashing the crystal bowl. She landed in an ignominious heap amid the jumble, her hands closed around the squirrel's tiny, furry body.

A shadow fell across her, and she hoisted herself up on one elbow to turn and look at the straight-backed figure looming behind her.

"Um, *bon jour, Mère*. I mean, Mother." Her mother disliked it when she called her *Mère*. Delilah's use of French—specifically, her *poor* use of French—drove her mother to distraction.

Her mother's dark, imperial eyebrow lifted. The frown on her face was both unmistakable and omnipresent. The Earl of Hilton stood to her right, an irritated smile on his smug face.

"She takes after her father, doesn't she?" He eyed Delilah down his haughty, straight nose. "Clumsy."

Lord Hilton had supposedly been Papa's closest friend. Ever since Papa died over ten years ago, the man had been hovering about Mother. Delilah had suspected for a while now that they were courting. He and his hideous son, Clarence, had begun coming around more and more of late. Delilah guessed they were interested in money, and unfortunately, her mother had a great deal of it. Her uncle was the earl now, but Papa had provided generously for both her and her mother's future.

Mother lifted her chin, her lips pursed. It was never good when her lips pursed. "This creature looks like my daughter, but I'm not certain I wish to claim her at the moment."

Delilah scrambled to her feet. Her hair had come out of the topknot and a large swath of it covered one eye and half of her mouth. Her grip still tight on the squirming squirrel, she tried to blow the hair away from her face, but the swath simply lifted momentarily and fell back into place.

Mary and Rose, the housemaids, had already begun cleaning up the mess she'd made. "I'm awfully sorry," Delilah said to them. They glanced at her, both offering sympathetic smiles. She'd been friends with them for an age, and they knew she was about to get a tongue lashing from her mother.

Mother's gaze fell to the squirrel, and she gave a long-suffering sigh. "What in heaven's name have you got there?" The countess's nostrils flared slightly as she glared at the squirrel as if it were a rabid rat.

Delilah clutched the little animal to her chest. *"L'écureuil,"* she announced, hoping the word for squirrel sounded more acceptable in French. Most things sounded more acceptable in French.

Her mother turned sharply toward the front door. "I am going to see Lord Hilton out. I'll give you five minutes to dispose of that *thing* and meet me in the salon. I need to speak with you." She whisked her burgundy skirts in the direction of the front door.

Delilah glanced about. The front door was the closest exit. She rushed past Mother and Lord Hilton to reach the door before they did as Goodfellow, the butler, opened it. She hurried out into the spring air and glanced around. The park was across the street. It would be the best place for the squirrel. She watched for carriages and then dashed across the muddy roadway and into the park, where she found a spot in the grass to carefully release the animal. "Take care, *Monsieur Écureuil,*" she said, as she leaned down and gently opened her palms against the soft, green grass.

She watched the squirrel scramble away to safety before she turned and rushed back across the road, further muddying her skirts in the process. *Mon Dieu*. Just another thing for Mother to disapprove of.

By the time Delilah reached the foyer again with a ripped, stained hem, she was breathing heavily and her coiffure had become even more unwieldy. At least the Earl of Hilton was gone. She quickly flipped the unruly swath of hair over her shoulder. Best to pretend as if she couldn't see it. She rushed into the salon and stopped short to stand at attention in front of her mother, who was seated, stiff-backed and imperious, like a queen upon a throne.

Mother eyed her up and down before shaking her head disapprovingly. "Take a seat."

Delilah lowered herself to the chair that faced her mother's. She'd learned long ago that if she kept her eyes downcast and nodded obediently, these sorts of talks were over much more quickly. Too bad she didn't have it in her to do either. "About the squirrel, I—"

"I do not wish to speak about the squirrel." Her mother's lips were tight.

"About the vase and the table, I—"

Mother's eyes were shards of blue ice. "I do not wish to speak about the vase or the table."

Poor *Mère*. She would have been beautiful if she weren't always so angry. Usually with Delilah. Her mother's blond hair held subtle streaks of white, her eyes so blue eyes they would have been heavenly if they weren't so hard. She had a perfect, patrician nose and lines around her mouth no doubt caused by years of frowning at her only child.

Delilah looked nothing like her. Lord Hilton was right. Delilah took after her father. She had Papa's dark brown hair and matching eyes. A butter stamp, they'd called her, meaning she looked exactly like him. Delilah was of medium height while her mother was petite. Delilah was exuberant and talked far too loudly and far too much, while her mother was always calm and reserved. Delilah was a failure on the marriage mart, while her mother (even at her advanced age of three and forty) had a score of suitors. Hilton was the most aggressive, and her mother's obvious favorite.

Delilah's mind raced. If Mother didn't want to chastise her about the vase, the table, or the squirrel, what could she possibly—

Delilah winced. "Is it about the donkey ears?"

Mother's eyes widened slightly with alarm. "Donkey ears?"

Oh, dear. Now was probably not the best time to tell Mother she'd been rehearsing a play for charity. The woman rarely approved of anything Delilah did, and joining the outrageous Duchess of Claringdon, Lucy Hunt, in a production of a play was certain to be another in a long list of things Mother disapproved of, even if they were performing Shakespeare's *A Midsummer Night's Dream*.

"Never mind," Delilah said in as nonchalant a voice as she could muster.

Mother delivered another long-suffering sigh. She touched one perfectly manicured fingertip to each of her temples. "I don't even want to know what you meant by that. But no, it's not about any of those things." Her mother's hands returned to settle motionless in her lap.

Delilah watched with awe. She'd never been able to master the art of sitting perfectly still. She also hadn't mastered the arts of speaking fluent French, being patient, pouring tea without spilling it, keeping her clothing clean and rip-free, or any of a number of other things she'd tried. And all of her shortcomings were a source of unending shame to her mother.

Delilah pressed her lips together, but she couldn't keep her slipper from tapping the floor. When would she learn it was always better to allow Mother to speak first? The conversation tended to be less incriminating that way. "What *would* you like to speak to me about, Mother?" she forced herself to ask in the primmest voice she could muster. Mother had always valued primness.

Mother straightened her shoulders and pursed her lips. "It's about your marriage."

A sinking feeling started in Delilah's chest and made its way to the bottom of her belly, where it sat, making her feel as if she'd swallowed a tiny anvil. She'd known this day would come, known it for years, but she had merely hoped it wouldn't arrive quite so ... soon.

"You'll be three and twenty next month," Mother continued.

A fact. "Yes, Mother."

"That is *far* beyond the age a *respectable* young woman should take a husband."

That depended upon what one considered respectable, didn't it? It also depended on whether one's goal was respectability. "Yes, Mother."

"You've spent the last five Seasons running about with the Duchess of Claringdon, playing matchmaker for other young ladies."

True. "Yes, Mother." Delilah managed to stop her foot from tapping, but her toes continued to wiggle in her slipper.

"You don't seem to have given so much as a thought to your own match."

Also true. "Yes, Mother." Was it her fault if it was much more diverting to find matches for other people than to worry about a courtship for herself? When she was a girl, she'd looked forward to being courted by handsome gentlemen. But that had been years ago, before she'd grown up to be entirely unmatchable. She'd always known she would have to try to make her own match eventually, however. Someday. Apparently Mother's patience was at an end.

"I daresay your friendship with Huntley hasn't been a good influence. He also refuses to make a match. And he's a duke, for heaven's sake. He'll need an heir someday."

Delilah winced. It was never good when Mother mentioned Thomas. The two could barely stand each other. "Thomas doesn't exactly believe in marriage."

"Yes, well, *you'd* better start believing in it." Mother's highly judgmental eyebrow arched again. "This is your *sixth* Season, and it's nearly over."

Yes, but who was counting? And why did Mother have to pronounce the word *sixth* as if it were blasphemy? She sounded like a snake hissing.

"I insist you secure an engagement this year," Mother continued. "If you do not, I shall be forced to ensure one is made for you."

Delilah shot from her chair. "No! Mother!" Her fists clenched at her sides.

Mother's brow lifted yet again, and she eyed her daughter scornfully until Delilah lowered herself back into her seat. She managed to unclench her fists, but her foot resumed the tapping.

Mother pursed her lips. "You fancy yourself the *ton*'s matchmaker, my dear. It's high time you made your *own* match."

Delilah took a deep breath and blew it out. Then she took another one for good measure. Aunt Willie had taught her that little trick when dealing with her mother. How Aunt Willie and Aunt Lenore, her cousin Daphne's mother, had grown up with Mother and been so different, so happy and nice and pleasant, Delilah would never know. The three sisters couldn't have been more dissimilar.

After the third steadying breath, Delilah forced herself to think. Marriage. Very well. This was actually happening. She would have to make a match by the end of the Season. She gulped. Next month.

"Of course, you'll have to find someone who is willing to put up with your ..." Her mother eyed her up and down again. "Eccentricities. But there are plenty of young men of the Quality who are in need of a hefty dowry. I suggest you set your sights on one of them."

Delilah blinked back tears. She refused to let her mother see her cry. She hadn't allowed it since she'd been a girl. When Papa died. That was when Mother had informed her that crying was for people who had no control over their emotions, something Delilah had always struggled with. Her emotions tended to immediately register on her face. That was just one of the many reasons she had always been a terrible disappointment to her mother. It was obvious, and had been for years.

But Delilah *had* always intended to make a good match. She had. She'd merely been ... distracted. Why, together, she and Lucy had made splendid matches for all of Delilah's friends. Lady Eleanor Rothschild, Lady Clara Pennington, and Lady Anna Maxwell. Those young ladies had made their debuts with Delilah, and one by one they'd been married off to charming, handsome, titled gentlemen of the aristocracy ... in love matches, no less.

"Don't misunderstand me," Mother continued, passing a perfectly manicured hand over her perfectly pressed skirts. "I don't expect you to make the match of the Season."

Delilah blinked. "The match of the Season?" Surely, her mother didn't mean—

"I've heard the Duke of Branville is looking for a bride this year."

Drat. That's exactly who her mother meant. And it was true. The Duke of Branville had long been the most coveted bachelor on the marriage mart. Until this year, he hadn't shown an interest in finding a bride. She and Lucy had already spent the better part of the Season avidly discussing his prospects. It was one of their favorite pastimes actually. "Yes," she murmured in response to her mother. "The Duke of Branville is certainly eligible."

Her mother's lip curled. "As I said, I've no expectation that you could secure an offer from the likes of Branville, for heaven's sake. No. I think someone a bit more, ahem, reasonable would be best." She sat up even straighter if that were possible. "To that end, I already have chosen someone for you."

Delilah's stomach performed a somersault. "Who?" Cold dread clutched at her middle.

"Clarence, of course."

Delilah's jaw dropped and her brows snapped together. "Clarence ... Hilton?"

Her mother directed her gaze skyward for a moment. "Of course, Clarence Hilton, who else?"

"Oh, Mother, no!" Delilah couldn't help the disdain in her voice. "I'm certain I can do better than Clarence Hilton."

"Oh, really?" Mother drawled, crossing her arms over her chest and regarding Delilah down the length of her nose.

"Yes, really." Delilah nodded vigorously. She'd rather marry a good-natured goat than Clarence Hilton. The man was portly, smelly, and rarely spoke, and when he did, he had nothing interesting to say.

"Very well." Mother stood from her seat and made her way toward the door. "I'll give you until your birthday to secure a better offer."

Delilah clenched her jaw. Her mother didn't think much of her. She certainly didn't think Delilah was capable of attracting a worthwhile suitor, and she obviously didn't think Delilah could attract anyone better than Clarence Hilton.

Anger bubbled in Delilah's chest. Normally, she did her best to keep it at bay. Anger was an emotion, after all. But sometimes, no matter how hard she tried, she couldn't keep such thoughts from throbbing in her brain. She was a butter stamp of her father in more ways than one, and the current way involved being madly stubborn and ridiculously determined once she set her sights upon something.

By God, Delilah would show her mother. She would prove to her that she wasn't the lost cause Mother thought. Besides, who better to make the match of the Season than she herself? She was an excellent matchmaker, wasn't she? She had done it before. More than once.

"You'd do well to remember that Clarence Hilton is the heir to an earldom," Mother intoned.

"I'm well aware." Delilah tried and failed to keep the sarcasm from her voice.

"Don't be impertinent. You truly believe *you* can secure an offer from someone with better connections than that?"

Delilah raised her chin and met Mother's glare. She would die trying. Because her mother had just issued a challenge of sorts, and unfortunately, Delilah—emotional, too-loud, eccentric Delilah—had never been able to pass up a challenge.

Besides, her odds of success had to be better than average. Her best friend, Thomas, was always talking about odds. Numbers leaning this way or that. He put great stock in them. Delilah rarely gave odds much thought, but now she had to believe they were in her favor. After all, Delilah had the infamous Duchess of Claringdon, Lucy Hunt, in her corner, and that woman was undisputedly the best matchmaker in the land. "Yes," she declared. "I believe I can."

"Fine." Mother paused in the doorway and turned to regard her daughter, a hint of disdain in her forced smile. "Do you have anyone in mind? Any prospects?"

Delilah straightened her shoulders. Her mother's lack of faith in her hurt, but it also made her resolute. Her birthday was the twenty-first of July. She had just over a month to accomplish her goal. Her perhaps overly insanely lofty goal.

"Yes, in fact." Delilah stood from her seat and met her mother's stare with her own highly determined smile. "I intend to secure an offer from the Duke of Branville."

CPSIA information can be obtained
at www.ICGtesting.com
Printed in the USA
LVHW051459040619
620111LV00003B/572/P